# 18 WHEELS
## RODEOS AND BULLS

# 18 WHEELS
## RODEOS AND BULLS

H.M.R. HART

*18 Wheels Rodeos and Bulls*
Copyright © 2019 by H.MR. Hart. All rights reserved.

No part of this publication may be reproduced, stored in a retrieval system or transmitted in any way by any means, electronic, mechanical, photocopy, recording or otherwise without the prior permission of the author except as provided by USA copyright law.

This novel is a work of fiction. Names, descriptions, entities, and incidents included in the story are products of the author's imagination. Any resemblance to actual persons, events, and entities is entirely coincidental.

The opinions expressed by the author are not necessarily those of URLink Print and Media.

1603 Capitol Ave., Suite 310 Cheyenne, Wyoming USA 82001
1-888-980-6523 | admin@urlinkpublishing.com

URLink Print and Media is committed to excellence in the publishing industry.

Book design copyright © 2019 by URLink Print and Media. All rights reserved.

Published in the United States of America
ISBN 978-1-64367-529-9 (Paperback)
ISBN 978-1-64367-528-2 (Digital)

17.04.19

# PREFACE

Sabrina Saunders now Sabrina Avery was the struggling single mom of a little boy named Jeremy. Sabrina used her skills as a truck driver and owner to pay the bills and make ends meet. While her loving widowed mother, Monica stayed at home overseeing the farm and taking care of Jeremy.

Sabrina's luck in love and money always seem to run short. In just one day everything changed and as it did, she made big changes in their lives as well. Having a big heart she stopped to help another driver. Next, she decided to step in and more than help her new friend. She also found a new family to share the wealth with. Now with her new love and family,Sabrina Saunders Avery gave birth to twins Matthew and Amanda while becoming the proud owner of a 5000 acre ranch. Sabrina knew that now being ranch owner, wife, and mom she would never lack for love. With her new found family Sabrina, Jeremy, and Monica soon moved to Texas.

Keep reading to find out what happens next as they all become a happy family 18 wheelers rodeos and bulls

# CHAPTER 1

It has been three years since Hope Ranch started gentling mustangs. Hope Ranch was also put back into a full operational ranch in all of its 5000 acre glory. TJ Avery and his wife Sabrina now the owners have decided to take on more responsibility. They have now decided to also start raising cattle again. Although they know Sabrina's mom Monica wanting to raise a garden for canning and vegetable sales they will need to hire more ranch hands.

This will also mean some of the acreage will need to be worked as hay and corn fields. In turn TJ will need to purchase more farm equipment with the spring season coming on fast. They will need to also sit down and discuss when and what will be needed to be done first.

Everyone is called to dinner and as everyone has eaten a full meal discussions begin. TJ starts out by saying, "Everyone as you know we have been talking about bringing cattle back to the ranch. Sabrina and I will be attending several sale barns in the next few weeks. Meanwhile we will need to check all the fences and fence off some property for crops and Monica's garden."

"TJ can I say something?"

"Yeah Teresa. What's on your mind?"

"Did you forget we promised to supply the livestock for the rodeo this year?"

"Oh yeah I did forget. Thank you! I guess this will mean we will definitely need to hire more ranch hands. Turning to Jose, the ranch hand TJ asked,"José can you help with that? I know you've been asking about some of your family members."

"Yes sir! Be glad to I will contact them when we're done here. I will also be needing help with their work visas."

"TJ we're going to bring José's family here. We will need to fix up the housing on the east side of the ranch."

"Sabrina that's a great idea this way they will be right here close. Will you and the ladies get that done? Also babe you will need to contact our lawyers for the proper paperwork for them."

"Sure TJ. I will also get him to draw up the rodeo contracts."

"I still say God sent me an Angel when he sent me you, Sabrina."

"Okay everyone if that's all I guess we all have a lot to do starting in the morning."

"TJ, did you forget we have two loads of mustangs coming in tomorrow morning?" Jose asked.

"Now as a matter fact I didn't forget José. JC and Jack have that covered already."

"Daddy, can I ride the fence lines was uncle Hoss in the morning? Please? I promise I will stay with him and do what he says."

"Hoss, do you mind if Jeremy rides with you?"

"No I don't mind. He can ride Charlie."

"Good. With all that settled now it's time we all call it a night. See you morning."

# CHAPTER 2

"Sabrina, please call the guys in for breakfast?"
"Sure Margie be glad to. Is TJ with them?"
"I think so. There was a problem with the second load of mustangs this morning so José called him out to thebarns."
"Thanks Marty you the best! I will have mom bring the kids down as well. They were almost dressed when I left them."
"Good morning Chris!"
"Good morning Sabrina!"
"Chris, I won't be here for lunch I am having lunch with Gary our attorney. We are going to go over the contract for the rodeo. They want us to take it over. I've been on the phone all morning with the rodeo association."
"Sounds like you know what you're doing."
"I hope so Chris. They will be giving us more of their bulls."
"Good morning Breezy!"
"Good morning TJ! Sweetheart can we talk in your office this morning before I go to lunch with Gary?"
"Sure babe! We will need to discuss a few things anyway. Now let's both have some breakfast."
"Morning mommy! Morning daddy!"
"Good morning baby girl. How is our Mandy this morning?"
"Great daddy butI'm hungry."
"Okay, sit down. I'm sure Chris will have your favorite chocolate chip pancakes." "Okay daddy. I love you!"
"Love you too Mandy."

"Breakfast was as always wonderful. Thank you Chris!"

"You're welcome Sabrina."

"Now if everyone will excuse us, TJ and I need to talk some things over. Hoss you have Jeremy today make sure he wears his helmet."

"Yes ma'am!"

"Hey kiddo! Can I have that hug and kiss before you go off riding today? "Sure love you mom!"

"Love you too Jeremy."

"TJ you know that I am meeting with Gary today?"

"Yes babe. Do you know who all do we need work visas for?"

"Yes TJ. I have them written down right here."

"Good they will be here in about three days."

"It will be handled by then TJ. Don't worry about it. We need to discuss the rodeo. They called this morning. Adam the president said he already talk to you."

"He did Breezy."

"What did he say to you?"

"He says he wants us to take over the rodeo and that you're the man for the job. You already more or less approved it. Is that true?"

"Yes Breezy I did."

"Okay then I will have Gary draw up the paperwork."

"Good. That will be settled then as well."

"Sabrina I need you to come to the Barns and approved some of mustangs for the rodeos."

"Okay I will after I get back from meeting with Gary. TJ there is an auction tonight in El Paso I hear they have put plenty of rank bulls. They are putting them up for auction. Do you want to go?"

"Yeah babe I think we should. By the way those four bulls came in this morning. Breezy they will need a lot of feed and TLC if they are going to go back to bucking."

"I will look them over when I come down to check out mustangs"

"TJ, TJ where are you?"

"Over hear by the soon- to- be new bullpens. What's up, Breezy? I'm going to see them 4 bulls. Then I will pick out the mustangs we need for the rodeo."

"Good! Let's get it done so we know what we have.

# CHAPTER 3

It has been three weeks since José's family came on board. With rodeo contracts signed, Sabrina called everyone to the main house for lunch. She has good news for everyone after lunch. She is only hoping to have a good lunch then she is about to give José and JC their citizenship papers. They are now both citizens of the United States.

"You're awful quiet Breezy?"

"No just thinking while I eat. I have a lot on my mind."

"Okay, spill it! You are never this quiet!"

"Okay TJ here goes. Chris bring in the cake. Congratulations!"

"Who are you congratulating?"

"Okay let me start with JC. As of eight o'clock this morning, you are now a full citizen of the United States of America. Here is your certificate. I had it framed for you. I hope you like the frame."

"I can't believe it! Is this real? I am now a citizen? I always dreamed of this but, I never thought it possible."

"Yes, it's real. Congratulations. Okay now for José first let me start by saying this is been very hard for me. I didn't even tell TJ. So here goes. José, you too are now a US citizen but that's not all. I want to give you a promotion. As you know we are going to be traveling a lot with the rodeo. Therefore I was thinking we need someone to oversee the ranch when we are gone. José, you have been here the longest and you know how we like things done. TJ and I already discussed it. He left it up to me. So as for now you will be our assistant ranch foreman and be getting a salary of $1000 a week. Also, we would like it if you and JC would move in here to the main house."

"TJ, Sabrina... I don't know what to say or even how to thank you both except by saying yes. I will do it! I plan to make you both very proud. Sabrina, you're the best thing that could've happened for all of us here at Hope Ranch. Now we have work to do. You guys only have two weeks to get ready. That is when we will pull out the first rodeo. Can we help while you get ready and practice?"

"Sure will! Everyone, José has a good point. Let's have some cake and then we will get started."

Now down at the stables Teresa is giving the children lessons. They are on their very own ponies that they are planning to take along. Matthew is being a trite Henri. He wants his pony, Spirit to run. While his sister Amanda is on her pony, Bell. She is just happy being on her pony; walking around and singing nursery rhymes.

"These two are total opposites, Sabrina! Will you please do something with Matt before he gets hurt?"

"Sure. Matthew James, if you keep that up you will be grounded and not be allowed to ride for two weeks. Now cut it out! If you get grounded you won't be able to practice. Then you will be left at home with grandma."

"Yes, mommy. I'll be good. Now where's Jeremy? I haven't seen him. Okay you should have them covered here now. I will go look for him."

"Jeremy, what are you doing in there?! Come on quietly. Come to mom." "Mommy, I'm okay he is my friend."

"Jeremy, that is the meanest bull we own! Your dad won't even get near him! Please, son. Come to mom?"

"Mommy, watch. He's not mean. We are friends. Come here. Give me kisses." The bull gently walks up to Jeremy and lets him kiss him on the nose.

"Sabrina, get him out of there! That bull will kill him!"

"No, I don't think he will TJ. The bull is gentle and quiet for Jeremy... so weird. Watch how he reacts to Jeremy||like they have a bond that is untouchable. This may do us a favor. If Jeremy continues to handle him at least someone will be able to stop his rage."

"Yeah Breezy. I guess but we won't let him in there alone anymore."

"Yeah TJ. I think you're right."

"Jeremy, come on I need to talk to you."

"Yes mommy. See you soon, love you Diablo. Be good boy so daddy can feed you. What mom?"

"Jeremy, dad says if you're going to work with him you can't do it alone. From now on daddy or I will be with you just in case."

"Okay mommy. I want you to anyway."

"Okay buddy. I will then Dad's busy helping with cat Now go and ride your pony Misty. You need to practice Jeremy."

Jeremy runs off to practice.

# CHAPTER 4

Sabrina walks into TJ's office mad as hell. "Thomas James! Do you have any idea what's going on down at thebarns? We pull out for Pecos in the morning. There are men that claim to know you down there. They are taking cattle prods to Diablo. Jeremy is in tears! The one who calls himself Lance pushed Jeremy down. They said you are okay with it?!"

"Breezy calm down I will handle this."

"You better because I am about to throw them off the property. When I do I will have them arrested. We do not treat our animals that way nor do we call our children snot-nosed brats. We agreed this would be a well-managed rodeo circuit.

"What in the hell do you boys think you are doing?!"

"Tommy boy long time, no see. We heard you had livestock here. We stopped by to check out the competition- the bulls that is until some bitch and a little snot-nosed brat that you must have working for you tried to stop us. If she wasn't such a bitch,she would be a hottie. I'd do her. Hell, I still might even do her just so I can knock her down a peg or two."

"Lance, let's get something straight! That woman has a name. Her name is Sabrina and she is my wife. The kid you knocked down and called a snot-nosed brat is my oldest son, Jeremy and that happens to be his bull. Your way out of line!"

"That bull will kill that kid!"

"Lance, you need to take your crew and go on to Pecos. If you don't, I may just let my beautiful wife, that you're not going to touch, have a piece of you. Even I know better than to mess with her when she's mad. NOW GIT!!!"

"Thank you T. J I knew in my heart you wouldn't put up with their crap. I Love you babe!"
"I Love you too Breezy!"
"Mommy, Daddy look. Diablo is lame. He can't hardly walk."
"Oh my god, T. J! Call the vet. We'll need to sedate him so we can see how bad he's injured."
"No Mommy come here. He'll let you if I tell him it's okay. Please he needs you NOW!!"
"Ok, ok. T. J, please still call the vet."
"Okay honey I will, straight away."

T. J has called the vet while Sabrina approached Diablo. "Easy boy I just want to see how bad you're hurt. I want to help you." Diablo lets her approach him. His head is down and you can see he's in a lot of pain. Sabrina immediately sees some wide-open gaping wounds. They're still bleedingprofusely. She works on stopping the bleeding. Diablo is dealing well with the pressure from Sabrina. Everyone is quite amazed. Everyone knows full well it's because Jeremy is staying with them. He's quietly singing songs to him while Sabrina works with Diablo.

A vet from El Paso Equine Medical Clinic has arrived. It's Tamara and she's very scared. She's been told horror stories about Diablo – everything from he's charged at another vet to he'd rather kill you than look at you. When she sees how badly he's injured and that he's doing great for Sabrinaand Jeremy she decides to take care of him. Jeremy manages to keep him calm. With that being said, Tamara sedates him. He has sustained enough cuts to need over 100 stitches. He also has a fractured bone in his front leg. He will be needing round the clock care & kept quiet.. That means Jeremy and Sabrina will have their hands full.

# CHAPTER 5

Now that the vet has gone and Diablo is settled for the night, T. J & Sabrina settle in to bed. They started talking.

"T. J, what are we going to do about Diablo? He's going to need me and Jeremy to keep him settled and treat his injuries. Also, he was supposed to be our prize bucking bronc. Now we're down a bull and we may have to change our half-time show. So now what?"

"I'm not sure. Let's sleep on it then talk in the morning."

"Okay. You're right this will give me time to game plan our next moves. Love you T. J"

"Good night. Love you,too."

Everyone is sitting down for breakfast the next day,

"Good morning all. T. J and I have been talking about what to do at intermission. Diablo is no longer an option for now. This means Jeremy and Diablo will not beperforming. Also, that puts us out a great bull. He was supposed to be our mystery bull –the big money bull. So for now, we will let the kids do their comedy act. Also, we will use a couple of calves, the sheep and the two mountain goats for the kids to ride. Now I know this adds a few more animals to the show but we have to put on a great show. So as soon as breakfast is done we will start loading for Pecos. Jeremy and I will be traveling back and forth for now. Diablo won't let just anyone take care of him. For now he's too badly injured to even travel. T. J will be staying with all of youand the animals at night. Jeremyand I will be back every morning. Pecos is a 3-day rodeo. Then we will move on to Van Horn,

Texas. Van Horn is a 4-day rodeo. After Van Horn, we will head back to El Paso. Okay that's enough for now. See you at the barns."

All the animals have been loaded and are heading for Pecos. With the C. B radios on channel 7 all seems to be going well when Sabrina chimes in that something is wrong with her rig. She starts to pull over when black smoke rolls out of the stacks. At this point she soon realizes she has lost all power. She barely makes it off the road and radios T. J to go on and unload. He'll need to come back and get the animals she's hauling. Being stubborn, he doesn't want to leave her. She demands that he go on and come back. She doesn't want the animals left on the trailer to long.

"T. J Please it's only about thirty more minutes until you get there. I do believe the engine has blown. If not, I know it's at least dropped some valves. We can't get lucky enough for it to be a blown turbo. So please just go. It will be easier for a tow company to just take the tractor back to the dealer in El Paso."

"Okay Breezy but I don't like it. I would rather be the one to wait while you take my truck and come back for me."

"I know but you can get it done faster."

"Okay, Breezy. Just don't do anything stupid like trying to fix it yourself here on the side of the road."

"It's beyond anything I can do."

"Okay. See you in a bit then."

Sabrina was in the sleeper birth getting caught up on paperwork she intended on doing once she got to Pecos and unloaded. She figured this way there wouldn't be any time wasted. She heard a knock on the door and looked at the clock. It's only been about thirty minutes so she knows it's not T. J or the tow company from El Paso. Sabrina sets her paperwork aside and gets up to see who it could be. She pulls the curtain back to see a black-haired young lady standing on the running board.

"Hello, my name is Sierra Chandler. Are you okay?"

"Hi I'm Sabrina Avery. Yes, I'm okay but I think we blew the engine. I'm waiting for a tow truck and another tractor to take this load on to Pecos. Are you headed to the rodeo?"

"Yes I am. Do you want me to wait with you?"

"You're welcome to if you like but I am okay. Hey if you're going to stick around, climb in."

"I think I will just for a bit. Looks like you have a load of horses on board."

"Yeah. These are the broncs and some of our personal horses."

"You wouldn't be related to the Avery bunch on a ranch just east of here, would you?"

"Well if being married to T. J qualifies as related then, Yes I guess I am."

"How did you pull that off? After the death of his one true love he turned into a scrooge. He vowed to never ride another bull, bronc, or horse ever again for that matter."

"Well, Sierra let's just say that after what happened the ranch went downhill and I stepped in to help. It took a lot of work and patience but I got through to all of them and now it's back in business."

"This sure is a beautiful truck, I can't believe the engine is blown."

"Well Sierra, believe it or not, this truck has been well cared for but it does have close to a million miles on the engine. This is the truck I was driving when I met the crew at the ranch. Hey there's T. J on the other side of the road now."

"Yeah Sabrina. I better go. See you at the rodeo."

"See you there. Be careful till then."

"I will."

# CHAPTER 6

"Hey Breezy! I see you and the animals are still here."

"Real cute T. J Like we had anywhere else to be."

"Did you call the tow company?"

"Yes T. J This isn't my first time to have a break down. They said they would be here in about an hour or so."

"Look, there they are now. I'll roll down the landing gear."

"Thanks sweetheart!"

"You're welcome, babe."

"Wow!! They said I would be picking up a tractor headed for the rodeo. I called someone to come get the trailer."

"Well obviously they didn't tell you I am loaded with horses or you didn't listen. Another tractor will not be necessary. No offense but, I don't trust just anyone with these horses or my other babies that are on board."

"Oh I'm sorry they did tell you a tractor."

"So next time do as you're told until you see for yourself what is needed. Now let's get this out from under the trailer so my husband can hook up."

"YES MA'AM!!"

"Don't be a smart ass or I will make some calls that will cost you an account." "Sorry!"

"Sabrina that was a little harsh, wasn't it?"

"No, because we aren't paying for someone we do not need. I know the game I drove tow trucks with my Dad when he was alive.

I never jumped to conclusions nor did I call for an extra truck until I knew for sure."

"Well Breezy, I just learned something else about my beautiful wife. You've never talked about life when your Dad was alive. Now I know how you got the love for driving. You got it from your Dad. Let me guess he's the one who taught you about mechanics as well?"

"Yeap, you are correct. I also got some of my temper from him. The orneriness came from Mom."

"No, not sweet Momma Monica?"

" Yes Mom."

"Driver, I'm hooked and ready to roll."

"No, not yet. Excuse me for a few T. J."

"Okay but watch your temper."

"Okay be right back. What are you doing checking your hook up. I don't want the truck damaged. Even if the engine is shot I will probably have another one dropped in it. Okay you are good to go. Take it to Kenworth of ElPaso. Your company has already been paid."

"Thank you!"

"You're welcome."

"Now let's get these animals on to Pecos. We're already behind a little."

"Yes dear, do you want to drive?"

"No T. J I thought I would get a turn on watching you drive."

"You're so bad Breezy. That's another thing I Love about you. You sure do know how to make a man feel good."

"Let's go T. J before these animals are held up longer and I end up pregnant again."

"As you wish, darling."

They have arrived at the stadium and all the animals are being settled in. Sabrina has her mom, Monica coming to pick her up later. She needs to settle some things at the rodeo circuit first. Sabrina will need to get all the entries logged in. She also needs to see to it that everything is up and running in the arena. Last but not least she wants to ride and let the kids ride and practice. With that being done, she and the kids will need to get back to the ranch. She and Jeremy still have to treat Diablo's wounds.

Now that everything is done at the rodeo Monica has arrived. Sabrina is looking for T. J so she can let him know they are leaving. She finds him in the office of the arena.

"Hi babe. Mom is here the kids and I are getting ready to head back."

"Hun, I really wish you didn't have to go but I understand. You and Jeremy have to treat Diablo."

"Yeah, afraid so. We will be back in the morning after we do his morning treatment "

"Okay babe. Love you,be careful."

"We will. Don't worry this isn't my first rodeo…Haha !

# CHAPTER 7

With the first few days out of the way, Sabrina and the children arrived at the arena on Saturday morning. Monica, Margie and Chris will be there before noon. Chris is putting together a great lunch for the crew. It will be a surprise for everyone. He knows how they all like his surprise dishes at lunch time. Sabrina and the kids are in the arena when Maria enters on her contest horse. Maria seems to be having issues handling him. Maria has no idea who Sabrina is when she got off her horse and approached them.

"You need to get those brats out of the arena and out of my way. I need to practice and my horse doesn't like ponies plus, I can't stand kids."

"Do you even know who I am?"

"Yeah the bitch I am going to whip if you don't leave."

"Oh okay. Hang on a minute."

"Yeah Breezy?!"

"Will you please come to the arena, Hoss and get the kids for me."

"Sure. What's up Sabrina? Are you okay?"

"Yes. I will be and I will explain later."

"Okay. Be right there"

. "Kids, wrap it up. Uncle Hoss is coming to get you."

"Okay Mommy we are."

"Hey Hoss! Thanks for coming."

"You're welcome!"

"I will be in there in a bit. We will talk when I get there." Sabrina whispers to Hoss," Who is that?" "

"Her name is Maria Sanchez. Why?"

"I will explain later. Thanks again. Now Matt you and your sister do what Hoss says."

"We will Mommy."

"Now that my children are out of ear shot,Maria! You have no idea who the hell you are dealing with! Or do you? Well since you threatened me let's see what you do now that the children are no longer here. What's wrong Maria? Aren't you going to back it up? Oh! I forgot your horse is in your way. You know even your horse doesn't like you. If you got rid of the spurs you mightget somewhere with him. You think you have to use force to get your point across. Well, you're terribly wrong. Now again do you plan to back that threat up? I didn't think so. Besides you're not worth it. I'll beat you at your own game tonight only without spurs or other vices. Gotta go now. The kids need me."

"Hey Hoss. Where are the kids?"

"With their grandma, Margie, and Chris. Chris is setting up lunch in the office. Now what was that about Breezy?"

"Well Ms Sanchez said a few rude things in front of the kids. She also threatened me. So I gave her the chance to put her money where her mouth is."

"Well did she?"

"No she didn't say anything at all. She'lllearned the hard way and I won't have to lift a finger. I will just have to out run her on Mara or maybe even both. Wa Key a has picked up some more speed as well. I can't wait to see what happens tonight."

"Sabrina, you do realize she and T. J have history?"

"WHAT?! You're telling me this now. Why wasn't I told sooner?"

Slow down. Last we knew, she was engaged to Lance. Hell, that makes it worse."

"Okay. I'll deal with it as the time comes. Patience on my part will get me a lot further. I still intend to win tonight either way."

"Sabrina he never went out with her. He ended up with well his belated love. Sorry I promised to never say her name again at least not at a rodeo."

"I understand Hoss."

"No, I don't think you do. I still think she had something to do with that bull getting out. I just can't prove it. Please be careful Breezy!"

"I will I promise."

"Good! Now let's go eat! I am starved."

"Hoss, you're always hungry."

# CHAPTER 8

With today being a long day, everyone is glad to see that the stands are almost full and the rodeo set to begin in thirty minutes. T. J enters the arena and takes the microphone to start the first announcements. "Good evening ladies and gentlemen. We want to welcome everyone to the rodeo. We have a lot in store for you tonight. There will be, wait a minute, what are you doing Bozo?"

"You said a lot in the store."

"No I didn't! I said a lot in store."

"Same thing you said the magic words. I like stores. I have money now where did I put it? Maybe it's in here. No, that's not it. Here, hold this I need to dig a little more. Here hold thattoo. No, that's not it. Hold this as well. Okay, I think I got it. Uh oh here comes my wife, Sassy. I think I better put that back she doesn't know I have her bag."

"Bozo, I am going to whip you good this time."

"Gotta go, T. J. See you."

"Now where was I? Oh that's right I was about to introduce the bulls. Oops I meant to say staff."

With everyone introduced and all the events half-way through, it was now time for intermission. Sabrina rode in on T. J's Buckskin. She has a cordless microphone hooked to her outfit.

"Good evening, everyone. We have a few future cowboys & girls here to show their stuff. We also have a chance for a few good boys and girls to try their hand at riding. Yes, I said riding. Now do you wonder what? Well, they will try their hand at some small bulls, goats and sheep. Yes, parents. It is perfectly safe. If you want, I will even demonstrate with my own children. All you have to do is bring them down to the south entrance and sign them up. While you do that Jeremy, Amanda, and Mathew will be doing their routine.

Now that the children are in the arena with J. C overseeing their ride, Sabrina goes looking for T. J. She quietly walks up to him but he doesn't see her. Maria is with him and she sees Sabrina. Maria wraps her arms around TJ's neck. Sabrina just walks away more pissed now than before. After the children are done riding she goes and gets them and tells her Mom she is not riding tonight. She has pulled from the barrel racing and will be ready to leave shortly. She then looks for Hoss and lets him know they are leaving. He wants to know why. She tells him she doesn't want to talk about it that he should ask T. J. Sabrina bids him a good evening.

"Okay Sabrina now that we're home and everything is done, spill it."

"Mom I thought I would be enough for T. J but obviously he finally got bored. I saw him at half-time and Maria had her arms around him. I think I will go get our other truck from the dealer then hook up to one of the old bull racks. But, I have to go get Mara, and Wa KeyA. Better yet I will have Hoss bring them home in the morning."

"Breezy, I think you need to talk to him and hear his side of it."

"Why? He didn't feel the need to tell me he had history with her. I had to hear it from someone else. I just need some time. Tell you what I will wait a week or two. I prefer to drive my own truck anyway."

"Okay that's fair."

The next morning the phone rings and it's Jose, so she answers. "Good Morning Jose."

"Good morning,Sabrina! I thought I would call and see if everything is okay. I missed seeing you before you left last night."

"Oh, I'm sorry. It was a very long day and the kids where tired. We left a little early. I didn't want you guys to lose concentrationso we just went ahead and left."

"Okay. Well we will see you later today then?"

"Well, about that… can you guys just do the children in the audience ride? I think we will probably stay home today. Diablo is acting like he is missing Jeremy. I also want the kids to get their rooms cleaned. They were supposed to all week but didn't so they need to. They knew what would happen if they didn't do it. I just think we need to get off to a good start at the rules. This rodeo is not the only thing they need to learn."

"Okay see you Monday then."

"Thanks Jose."

"Breezy who was that?"

"That was Jose. Mom I told him we wouldn't be there today. I told him the kids need to clean their room. Besides that was the deal. If they want to do this they have to keep their end of the bargain."

"You're right Breezy. I will make them get on it."

"Thanks Mom!"

"You're welcome."

# CHAPTER 9

It is now Monday and everyone will be pulling in soon. Monica and Chris have got this (?) together in the house. Teresa and Alfredo have gotten the barns ready for the incoming animalsThe twins are in their room watching a movie. (connect the next sentences here). Sabrina and Jeremy are out with Diablo. The vet is with them looking over his condition. She has given the all clear for him to travel with the promise that he will be resting and not doing rodeo work. Also that Cleaves Veterinarians will see to him within twenty-four to forty-eight hours after arriving. She agrees to all of it and the vet agrees not to tell where she is going.

The first load is arriving with Hoss driving. He get out and the ranch hands greet him to unload. Sabrina goes out to see who it is and what animals have arrived. She sees Hoss and goes over to him. "Are you done or is this your first load?"

"My first load. Seeing how there is another trailer and animals there to bring home."

"Okay. I thought as much. I wouldn't have been any help anyway. Remember mine is in the shop?"

"Oh yeah. I kind of forgot."

"How did you do?"

"I rode second place behind T. J."

"Oh okay. I was hoping you would do better. As far as I'm concerned, you ride better…just my observation.

Hoss has worked his way into the house." Well hello Margy, Monica."

"Hello Hoss. How is everything going in Pecos?"

"It's almost all packed up, Margy. Can I asked you two a question?"

"Yes but, it doesn't mean we will know the answer."

"I only hope one of you do. Do you know what's bothering Sabrina?"

"Yes we both do but we vowed to stay out of it. Go ask her she may tell you." "Okay I will then."

"Hoss don't you need to get moving?"

"Yes Breezy. Is the trailer empty?"

"Looked like it to me."

"Breezy, what's wrong with you? Did one of us do something to upset you?"

"You could say that and then some. I had my heart ripped out and handed back to me. I swore that after James hurt me I wouldn't let it happen again. I'm such adumbass."

"Don't say that. You're not dumb."

"Yes I am. I let someone in and gave my heart away. Now I have three children and I am back in the same boat as before. I don't want to talk about this anymore."

Back at the rodeo, TJ looks for his wife, "Where is Sabrina?"

"She's still at the ranch. T. J I don't know happened here Saturday but I do know she is very upset. She said something about getting her heart ripped out again. She even called herself adumbass."

"Hey boss. Can I say something?"

"Sure if it helps."

"Maria is up to no good, I told her she didn't have anything to worry about. Someone told her that you and Maria have history. She said, if it's nothing to worry about why didn't he tell me about it." "Nonetheless, why didn't someone say something before now?"

"I tried to convince her that she's all that matters to you but she wouldn't budge on the thought or idea."

"Thanks. At least I know what I am walking into now.

Okay everything is loaded let's head back to the ranch. If Sabrina and I are behind closed doors once we're home, please don't disturb."

"Not a problem, boss. We will steer clear."

"Thank you that will mean a lot to me. I am going to try to get back in her good graces."

"Good luck big brother! You're going to need it."

"Thanks Hoss. Now, let's roll.

## CHAPTER 10

It is now Wednesday and Sabrina has managed to avoid T. J at cost. She decides to go talk to him. She sees he is on the phone and decides to wait quietly until he is finished. She can't help but overhear who he is talking to. "

Yes, Maria the next event is in El Paso. You will just have to see me then. No, I can't right now."

Sabrina runs out crying. She goes to where her Mom is in the den.

"Mom, I am leaving immediately."

"Stop. What happened?"

"I will tell you later." She hugs and kisses her Mom and walks out. Sabrina then tells Margy to pack up some of the kids' clothes and she will be back for them.

Meanwhile T. J had seen her run out and hung up to go talk to her. He can't seem to find her. So he goes to Monica who is with Margy.

"Okay I know you have seen my beautiful wife. Can you tell me where she is?"

"No because we don't know. Just that she said to pack a few things and that she would be back."

"Okay then I will wait right here with you."

"T. J what's going on? She will not tell us anything?"

"I am not for sure about it exactly but I do have an idea though."

"Okay. Spill it. What? I think she thinks I am seeing a lady by the name of Maria."

"Why would she think that?"

"I think she saw Maria hug me on Saturday. Then she just heard me on the phone with her."

"Well yeah T. J I guess I can see why she would think that."

"Gee Thanks, Margy."

Sabrina comes back from the dealer after purchasing a new Kenworth. She has just hooked it up to her bull rack and was loading it. Once loaded she called the house and asked her Mom to quickly bring the kids and their stuff to the cattle barn. Monica Agreed. As she puts the kids in the truck, T. J approached. Diablo was loaded and so were the horses and ponies. It was just a matter of pulling out.

"Sabrina please talk to me. Please don't go!"

"I have to I can't let the kids see you with that snob."

"But Breezy it's not what you think."

"I know what I heard and saw. If you really want her and her you then don't let us stop you. I gotta go. Talk to you later. Goodbye Thomas."

Sabrina pulls out and heads east. She plans to run I-10 to I-20 then cut north out of Dallas. She will need to call David her old boss from Cincinnati. She's hoping her place in Ohio hasn't been rented out again lately. The kids are settled in the bunk watching a movie. The phone rang it was Monica calling."

Hi Mom what's up?"

"I was worried so I thought I would give you a call."

"Mom, we haven't been gone long."

"I know. It just sunk in that you guys are gone. Where will you be?"

"Mom, I know T. J is beside you and he's the one who really wants to know."

"Okay you know me to well."

"You are absolutely correct. Don't do it again or you will never know. I love you Mom but I gotta go."

Sabrina calls David and her small farm is still sitting empty. So she makes arrangements to get it together when they get there. Sabrina also calls a veterinarian she knows that will come check on Diablo's well being.

"Well T. J I told you she was smarter than the average woman. Plus you have to remember how bad she was burned by James."

"I do remember. I was there for her when things got bad."

"I know but, I also know how she thinks. She'll calm down and think about things then she'll call. I know she will be okay. She has her babies with her that includes the animals. They will be what keep her from doing anything stupid."

"Okay I guess you're right. But, I don't have to like it. Do you have any idea where she might go?"

"Truthfully?No! She could be headed to North Carolina, Michigan, Kansas, Colorado, or even Ohio. She knows people all over the country. I learned years ago not to chase her. She'll just run farther,faster,and harder.

"You know her best. We'll give her a little time."

## CHAPTER 11

It has now been almost a month and T. J still hasn't heard from Sabrina. He just manned up and kept on going with the rodeo. Even though he hasn't, heard Monica has. A few other people also know what's going on as well.

Diablo has completely healed and is doing well for Sabrina and Jeremy. Amanda and Mathew have also been able to get in with him. All the kids are doing well in their training with Sabrina's undivided attention. David and Kendra comes every Sunday and takes the kids to church with them. Sometimes Sabrina joins them. On the last week of May she has decided to let the kids go to bible school which is in two weeks. The rodeo will be in town the last weekend of May.

Now with the children in bible school and the rodeo pulling in today it only being Wednesday, Sabrina rented a car to slip in and see a few of the ranch hands. She is hoping things are a little better but sheisn't counting on it. She sees the kids off and has made arrangements with David to keep the kids tonight. They will go to David and Kendra to spend the night. They are so excited about it. Arriving at the stadium, Sabrina notices her Mom and Hoss right away.

"Hi Mom!Hi Hoss!"

"Sabrina you look good. Where are the kids?"

"They are at bible school this week. I made arrangements with a friend to keep them so I could come see you guys."

"Where are you staying?"

"Here and there. Just around. I had to place Diablo at a large animal hospital for a bit. He's doing great now though. It's not easy trying to get a place to stay with a mean bull in tow."

"I bet not. Are you planning on coming back to the rodeo or even the ranch any time soon?"

"I don't know yet. Now enough with the 20 questions or I will get in the car and leave."

"Okay I get the hint. Now let's go see a few other people."

"Okay, let's go."

"Hey has everything been okay so far?"

"Yeah but T. J has been a major asshole. We all know why but it still doesn't excuse his rude remarks."

"Well, tell you what I am going to stay in the shadows just to see how bad he is."

"Would youplease?"

"Sure. I will need to see if Kendra would mind keeping the kids an extra day or so. Don't let too many people know I am here."

"I won't tellanyone.""

"Good that works."

Sabrina is staying back in the shadows listening when she hears TJ barking orders. "Jose what did I tell those idiots about the bulls being on one side and the broncs on the other? Are they trying to get someone badly hurt or even killed? Now fix this! "

"Yes Boss!"

"Where the hell is that worthless brother of mine? Better yet where is J. C? I sent them to bring in more gates. I thought they provided that for us?"

"T. J they do but not for our personal stock. They're not tall enough."

"Oh! Well excuse me for asking. I'll be in my truck if anyone should need me."

"Okay boss."

"Mom, Hoss I'll handle this he is not going to go on treating our staff this wayHello Jose."

"Sabrina! Thank God you're here. Do I have a lot to tell you."

"Don't bother I just heard and I am getting ready to bring T. J down a peg or two. I just wanted to saythank you, I am Sorry for his attitude. Keep up the good work and see you soon."

"Oh I almost feel sorry for the boss man now." "Don't. He doesn't deserve any pity."

"I did say almost."

"Yeah you have a good point. Good job Jose."

"By the way, will you be riding this weekend?"

"I doubt it. I will explain later."

"Okay. Just glad to see you."

"Same here."

# CHAPTER 12

Maria sees T. J get in his truck so she goes and knocks on the door. He doesn't answer at first, so she knocks again. He finally answers. "What do you want?"

"I just thought you may want some company."

"No I don't. I would like you to leave."

"But Tommy, I hate seeing you so upset all the time. I could help you relax a bit."

Absolutely not!Now get out of my truck and leave me alone."

"Okay but if you change your mind, you have my number." She gets out when Sabrina comes around the corner and sees her.

"Well I see the bitch with the brats is back. What are you doing stalking us?"

"No, not hardly. What do you think you're doing getting out of that truck?"

"That's none of your business, you stuck–up bitch."

"I think you are terribly wrong about that."

"We'll see."

"Yes we'll see for sure." Sabrina starts to walk past her when she grabs her arm. T. J has the window part way open in the bunk when he hears Sabrina. "Get your nasty hand off of me, you nasty lot lizard."

"What the hell is a lot lizard?" Sabrina chuckles. T. J can't help but laugh. "Yes it means you're a stupid horror!"

Maria then swings on Sabrina. Sabrina ducks then the fight begins. Sabrina delivers a left then a right punch getting Maria in the gut then the nose. T. J steps down out of the truckas Hoss and Jose come running."Okay you two that's enough," T,J says.

"What are you talking about? I just stood up for us. She swung first."

"Okay, still it's over."

"Okay I am done with her butnot with you. Get in the truck we are going to have a good long talk. First if you ever put your hands on me again you better have your life insurance paid up in full. Okay in the truck now."

"Damn I locked my keys in the truck."

"That's okay I have a set."

". Let me. Well, get out of the way."

"Yes ma'am!"

"Don't ma'am me. We talked about that a long time ago."

"Okay I take it this isn't a make- up visit?"

"Depends on what you have to say."

"Now that we are in the truck let's get in the bunk."

"No T. J not quite. Sit down."

"Okay. What is on your mind?"

"First, what was she doing in the truck? Then if I believe you, I will tell you what else is on my mind."

"Well she thought I would like some company. I told her that I don't and to get out. Then she tried smoothtalking me. I told her I wasn't interested, to get out and leave me alone. So she got out but not before she made it known she is still available. Then I said loudly to get out. Okay now on to other things on my mind."

"Before you say anything, I heard what you said about your brother, Hoss. Like what? You called him worthless. Then you wanted to know where J. C was. When you were told, you had a rude attitude about that as well. So what's up with the attitude lately?"

"I'm sorry. I guess I didn't realize I was coming off like that."

"Well, I don't like it and I am sure the staff don't either. You need to apologize to everyone."

"Yeah, maybe you're right."

"No, not maybe. You know I am. If I heard it then, just think how it makes them feel. How would you like it if it was you who was talked to and treated that way?"

"Yeah now that you put it that way, you are right. I will do it first thing in the morning."

"No! I think it needs to be done tonight."

"Okay. You sure it can't wait?"

"Positive. Everyone needs to know you have their back."

"Okay after we are done talking."

"Then we are done for now."

They both get out of the truck and went looking to round up everyone When they have, everyone met in the main office. "Hey all. I need to say that I am sorry I have been a jerk to all of you. I hope you can forgive me. I also wanted to tell you how proud I am of the crew we have. You have all been doing a great job. Then you still manage to ride and rodeo to boot. By the way I know everyone is wondering who is winning so far for the circuit well I think I'll make you wait til Friday night to find out."

"Oh boss, come on. Don't keep us in suspense."

"No, it can wait. Besides, you don't want to think I am cheating. I thought if Sabrina wouldn't mind I would have her go over the numbers again."

"Okay, we'll wait then- only because we know she is fair."

"That is all for now".

"T. J, Sabrina there was an ambulance just here. They took Maria to the hospital. She says she's going to sue the rodeo. She also says to have T. J come to U. C hospital. She said the bitch busted her up bad and she is going to prove it. She says she was pregnant and is losing your baby."

"Hold on a minute. I have never had anything to do with her. So if she is, it's not mine. Also, she wasn't hurt that bad. She walked off pissed Plus, we all seen it. She threw the first punch, Sabrina just defended herself. That was over 2 hours ago. Plus it's all on tape. We have cameras on the trucks. Plus, there are cameras on the trucks here. Also, there are cameras throughout the stadium. So I am sure once the police have a look at the footage, they will see the truth. Sabrina, will you call the police for me?"

"Be glad to."

The police arrive and all the videos have been gone over. They see the whole thing. It also shows Maria ramming herself into walls, fences, even punching herself in the stomach. The police thank them then make reports and leave them to their animals. "Well I guess that handled that situation. Now T. J I think we need to go finish our talk."

"No Sabrina. I just saved your butt. I think that should say it all."

"No, not quite. We still have a few things to talk about."

"Likewhat?"

"There goes that guilty attitude again. You tell me what? I'll be in my truck."

"Well, with that attitude you will be there alone."

"Guess I better get going anyway. I have a long drive ahead of me." "You mean that don't you?"

"Yeah I do as long as you're being a jerk."

He just walks off toward the truck leaving her with Hoss, and Jose.

"Do you really have a long drive ahead of you?"

"Jose, it seems like it's farther away than Texas."

"Well, we were hoping you would be back to run Friday Night."

"Well, even if I was here Friday, I couldn't ride."

"Why? You worked so hard for this."

"I just can't take a risk right now. The kids are depending on me. Besides I don't have my horses here."

"Okay. I guess maybe you should get back to the kids."

"Yeah well this time I will at least go tell that jackass of a man T. J bye."

"Good luck."

"You're a smartass, Jose. I will win. I always do."

"Now that's the Breezy we know and love. Get him girl." "Be seeing you guys later."

Sabrina walked away. "Hoss, what do you think she meant by she couldn't ride? She couldn't take the risk? I'm not sure you."

"Don't think… do you? Nah..no way! She couldn't be?"

"Well. maybe. Nah no way. Monica would have told us."

"Not if she doesn't even know."

"You're grabbing at straws. Maybe but that would be one way to get them back together."

"overheard that and you boys need to stay out of it."

"But Teresa they are perfect for each other."

"Yes but if anyone interferes and they are wrong, they could be out of work."

"Okay. We will butt out for now butif we're right, you owe use."

"Oh so you want to bet on it?"

"Yes I do. If I am right, you will marry me before the end of summer."

"Okay. If you're wrong, you will get down on one knee and propose before the season ends.

"You're on."

## CHAPTER 13

Sabrina is standing outside T. J truck. She has a lot to say to him but she doesn't know where to start. She decides to take the chance. She unlocks the door and climbs in. "T. J are you awake?"

"Yes. Just lying here hoping that this isn't a dream."

"No it's real. I am here."

"Please Breezy come back here with me. I still have things I need to tell you."

"Can it wait?"

"No. I have to get things off my chest."

"Okay. But come back here with me and tell me."

"Okay sure. But you have to hear me out."

"I promise Bree, I will."

"Thank you."

"Here I am. Please hug me before I start talking."

"Consider it done."

"Okay, thanks. Now, I wanted that hug because you might get mad."

"Not much can make me mad, Bree."

"Okay then here goes."

"T. J, I may sometimes seem totally trusting and confident in our marriage – for the most part, I am."

"What do you mean by that remark?"

"Stop! That's what I mean. You won't even let me talk Anymore. You just got totally rude. So I am going to finish whether you want to hear it or not. Back in Peco's, Maria came into the area and demanded I get those brats out of her way. So quietly I had Hoss come get them. I gave her anearfull and planned to show her who was the better horsewoman. I left and came to eat lunch. Then as the day went on, I decided to get going to treat Diablo. When we arrived back the next day, the kids rode, of course, then I came to find you. Well I did butyou didn't see me because she had herself wrapped around you. So I left. After being told you two had history and I couldn't get five minutes of your time to ask about it. I began to think if you two had history and there was nothing to it. Why didn't you tell me? So I was hurt that I honestly thought we had no secrets but here was one.

    I got mad and was planning to leave Monday around noon. Monica and Marge talked me out of it. So I stuck around with the intent to come talk to you about all of it before El Paso. Then, when I came to talk to you I heard you on the phone with her. So that's when I decided it was time to think things over on my own and to spend some well overdue time with the kids. So I went to the barns and loaded up. That's when I had the children packed up and brought to me. That's when you came out begging me not to go. That was the most time you spent in months wanting any part of me or the children. Now, take a minute and think about what I just said. Then you can say something."

    Sabrina doesn't get any answer she looks over then notices he's fast asleep. So with tears in her eyes she gently covers him up then quietly gets out of the truck and gets in the car and leaves. She finds herself crying as she is heading back to towards farm. As she gets on the expressway headed north she has merged over to the middle lane. Right around Hopple Street, a drunk driver is coming the wrong way at about 90mph. He meets her head- on.

    Sabrina is trapped. The engine has came in the front and on her. The steering wheel and the seat belt have her pinned in. Her head hit the driverside window and rendered her unconscious. She starts to regain consciousness but can't move. She can't even reach her phone nor can she feel her legs. Then she thinks *Oh my god! My baby. What about my unborn baby?* She soon hears sirens. She knows help is on the way. Oh god! She doesn't even know where she is or what happened. What does she tell the medics. *Just tell them to please save the baby* she thinks out loud. Someone hears her before she loses consciousness again.

As the medics arrive so do the police at the same time. Witnesses fill the police in as the interstate is shut down. Others have made medics aware of the situation of Sabrinaand what they heard her softly say before she got quiet again. They assess everything before they get started. Once they can get to her enough to just check her for a pulse, they realize they have one that's very weak. They start cutting into her, until the jaws-of-life can arrive. Once there they rapidly work to get her out. As soon as Sabrina was out,they continue to work on her. Realizing the only hope for her and the unborn child is life flight.

The helicopter lands and Sabrina is loaded where an on- board life flight doctor takes over. She still hasn't regained consciousness. They check to see if the fetus is still alive. The baby seems to be doing very well. Sabrina still has a very weak pulse. They land at University Hospital and Sabrina is admitted right away in I. C. U. She soon undergoes brain scans along with oxygen and numerous I. V lines. It will be all up to her now whether her body pulls out of it. They don't even know if she stopped breathing or not. That could mean lots of damage to her and possibly cost her the fetus. Hopefully they will know more by morning.

As the sun comes up, T. J's awakens to notice he went to sleep. Now he totally feels like crap because he went to sleep and didn't finish hearing what Sabrina was saying. He gets dressed then gets out of the truck. He goes looking for someone and finds Hoss. "Did Sabrina say anything before she left."

"No. We thought she was still with you."

"No. I went to sleep while she was trying to tell me what she thought and how she felt. I know I screwed up again."

"Hey, did you guys hear about the drunk driver that was going the wrong way on the interstate last night?"

"No. it's not our concern. I know Jose, you always listen to or watch local news so you know the weather. Okay also so you can learn some about the people from all over the United States. Bravo was anyone killed?"

"No. But the lady he met head-on was trapped and had to be air lifted to the hospital. They say she is in critical condition."

"Now onto what I was asking. Did anyone see Sabrina before she left?

"You mean she didn't stay?"

"No or I wouldn't be asking. I guess I will have to try calling to see if she will accept an apology. Then I will have to spend more time with just me and her. I know that was one thing she said before I went off to sleep. Before anyone says anything. I know I am such a major screw up."

"T. J as your brother, in your defense you was pretty tired. We have all been pushing pretty hard. I am sure you will figure out a way to make it up to her."

"I hope she will give me a chance." He calls and as he figures no answer.

As everyone has now gone to breakfast and are waiting for their food, the police walk in. "Is anyone here the husband of Sabrina Sanders Avery?"

"Yes sir,I am. This isn't in regards to Miss Sanchez? I thought that was handled."

"No, sir. You are needed at U. C Hospital."

"What's going on? What's wrong?"

"There was a bad wreck on interstate 75n last night. I am afraid to be the one to tell you, your wife was badly injured. You are needed to make some major decisions."

"No, god! No! I can't lose her. Not now. God, please tell me it isn't so."

"Mr Avery, do know how to get there?"

"No!"

"Can we give you a ride?"

"Yeah, sure. What's the name of the hospital again?"

"University of Cincinnati Hospital."

"Thank you. Go on T. J. We will be right behind you. We will pay the bill then leave.

"Okay."

# CHAPTER 14

Now that he has been at the hospital for a long while, T. J starts pacing the floor waiting to talk to the doctor. Everyone walks in, Teresa goes up to him and gently says, "T. J calm down. It will all be okay."

"Then why haven't they came out here to talk to me? Why can't I go back with her? Why won't they let me see her? She is my wife. They asked for me to come. I am here now and they make me wait."

A minister walks in an offers to pray with them and show everyone where the chapel is. "Yes please pray for her but for now until we know more, leave us alone."

"Okay I will. I will check back later today."

"That would be great. Thank you Pastor John."

The doctor walks in. "Hello. I am Doctor Meyers. I am the main doctor over Mrs. Avery. Know that I am not the only doctor. We are working as a team to oversee her care. Now first, who is her husband?"

T. J reaches out his hand and introduces himself as Thomas Avery. "Everyone calls me T. J for short."

"Have you been told what happened?"

"Only what the police know."

"Okay then. You know about the wreck and that it was bad?"

"Yes I do."

"Now can I have a word with you in private?"

"What you have to say, you can say in front of them. We are all family here."

"Well okay here goes. Sabrina came in with a very weak pulse. We thought maybe she was brain -dead. After an M. R. I of the brain,we found out that that is not the case. There is some damage due to head trauma but for now we will not know how much until she regains consciousness. That brings us to another problem. We will need to know what you would like us to do about the unborn fetus."

"What are you talking about?"

"You mean you didn't know? She's 4 to 4 ½ months pregnant. Do you want to know what she is carrying?"

"Yes by all means."

"She's carrying a healthy girl. The baby seems to be like her mom, a true fighter.

Here's what we are up against. If she doesn't regain consciousness in the next 72 hours,we may have to terminate the pregnancy. The longer she is unconscious the more the baby drags from her, the more damage can be done. It can include tearing her body down beyond repair. Meaning, at that point in order to just save one could mean lifesupport. Now you will have time to discuss it and make a final decision. I will leave you alone now to talk things over. We will need to know soon though."

"Can I see her?"

"Sure. Follow me".

WhileTJ is with Sabrina,Hoss calls the ranch and tells Margy what has happened. They will be in on the next flight out. A young lady comes in an asks about Sabrina's condition. When they tell her, she tells them what she heard Sabrina say and that she was at the scene of the accident. "

I'm sorry I didn't catch your name."

"Oh! I am so sorry. I am Chloe Augustine. I saw it from the other side of the road. I knew I had to stop. I got out of my car and jumped the guardrail. I knew it was bad. To be honest, I was surprised to hear a voice. I thought sure she would be dead. I didn't think anyone could have lived through that. I told the police everything and gave them my info. The problem is when I called to asked about her they wouldn't give me any info. So I came to find out for myself.

"We are so glad you stopped. Were you able to comfort her at all?"

"Well I did stand and sing Amazing Grace to her until help got to her. I am not sure if she even heard me but at least I tried."

"Thank you. Anything you did, I am sure was a huge helpeven if you didn't feel like it did.

"You're right. She is one tough cookie. We know in our hearther and this baby will pull through. I think once T. J is told what she said before she lost consciousness he won't let them take the baby."

"Can I stay? I really don't have anywhere to be until Monday evening. I would like to help all of you in any way I possibly can."

"Sure. You are welcome to stay with us."

"Thanks I appreciate it."

"You are welcome."

T. J. is sitting with Sabrina. He tells her he loves her. Even if she doesn't hear, he explains, "Breezy there has only ever been two women that I love. Katy was the first. You know all about her. You helped me get her moved to the cemetery at the ranch. The other one is you and only you. I promise youbaby, just pull through this and I will always be by your side. I would asked why you didn't tell me you're pregnant again. Maybe you did but my sorry ass went to sleep. Sweetheart, I took it for granted that things were fine. I should have listened. Please baby, wake up!I don't want to have to make a decision like the one I am facing."

A nurse comes in to check her vitals and change the I. V bag. T. J excuses himself. He then goes to the waiting room where everyone is. Hoss speaks up first, "T. J this is Chloe. She was at the scene of the wreck. She stayed with Sabrina until she was air lifted."

"Was she conscious while you were with her?"

"Only long enough to hear her say someone 'Please save my unborn baby.' Then as we could here sirens she got quietso I started to sing to her. I don't know if it was any help but I sang anyway. I didn't want her to feel all alone."

T"hank you Chloe I'm sure she probably did. Hey Hoss."
"Yes big brother. Where is Jose?"
"He went down to have a smoke."
"Okay someone will need to be there to run things at the rodeo. We have talked about it. Around 3p.m J. C and Jose will be heading to the stadium for the evening show. They will stay the night then after morning feed they will be back here. Where is Teresa?"
"She went to the airport to pick up Monica and Margy."
"Who called them?"
"We all were in on it but I made the call."
"Why did you do that?"
"Are you forgetting Monica is Sabrina's mother?
"You're right I'm sorry!"
"I understand big brother. She'll pull through she's tough Besides,we're all here and praying for her.

# CHAPTER 15

Monica and Margy are now walking in the door at the hospital after the plane has landed. Teresa was sure glad shedrove, Monica is on overdrive. She wanted to know about her daughter. As they are waiting on the elevator, David and his wife have also arrived . The children has been left with the pastor of their church. They all step on the elevator together. David soon realizes who is on the elevator with him. He pulls Monica to him in a big bear hug.

"Hello Davey."

"You know Monica you're the only one that ever got away with calling me that."

"I know. I do it to aggravate you."

"This is our floor."

"Yes it looks like it."

They are now in the waiting room with T. J and the rest of the crew.

"T. J what's the last word you got on Sabrina?"

"Well, she's still unconscious but seems to be holding her own. I was just in with her again. They had me leave so they can take her down for more test. The doctors are stumped that she hasn't gotten any worse or better."

"She'll pull through this T. J. She has to. We all need her."

"Well Monica, Margy give us a hug we have to get back for the rodeo. Before you ask, we will be back in the morning."

"You boys better or you will have two mad women to deal with."
"Yes Ma'am. We understand."
"See you in the morning then."

"Monica did you know she is pregnant?"
"She is what?"
"You heard me- pregnant."
"No. How far along? She better not have been riding and you knew about it. I may have been totally in another world but you know better."
"I just found out myself."
"Damn I should have caught on. She made a comment about knowing better than to trust another man. Then she said 'oh well here we go again single mom.' Left raising another child with the three she already has. In her defense she thought you and Maria had something between you. One thing I will say is she loves her children."
"You know, Monica you're right. I can understand her thinking that. Also she is a great Mom. I swear on Katy's grave there never was nor will there ever be anything between Maria and I."

The doctor comes in. "We have good news. so far there is no brain damage. The bad news is there is a tremendous amount of other damages. We won't know how much until she regains consciousness."
"Okay what could we be looking at."
"Well it's possible she have lost all feeling of her legs or worse. I can't say until she comes to. I still feel this unborn fetus could still cost her her life."
"Well, doc I have decided they say you're the best around. Now if you truly are then you will prove itIt's your job to save them both. So the answer is no you can not take our unborn baby."
"Okay then guess I have my work cut out for me."
"Yes you do."

"T. J that was a little harsh, don't you think?"

"No. All I continue to hear is how he wants me to let him terminate the pregnancy. I am sorry I don't believe in that anyway. Plus didn't you understand? Chloe said the last thing she said was please save her baby. So I do not feel that was harsh, just the opposite to polite. So Marge as much as you know I love you. Please don't ask me something like that again."

"I won't andI love you too, T. J."

"Good evening ladies and gentlemen! We would like to start by asking you for a few moments of your time. As some of you here may know, yesterday morning there was bad wreck on interstate 75n. A drunk driver was headed the wrong way on the freeway. He was running a speed of greater than 85mph when he hit another vehicle. Well, the beautiful young lady driving the other vehicle is now in critical condition. She is also the big boss to this rodeo. She is also 4 ½ months pregnant. So please let's bow our heads in prayer." After the prayer "Now thank you and let's get on with the show."

Now that the rodeo has ended itslast show in Cincinnati on a Sunday evening, a security guard approaches Hoss. "Mr. Hoss, can I please speak to you?"

"Sure. Is everything okay.?

"Yes it's great. We didn't want to offend anyone but the audience approached us. They had passed around hats and took up collections for Mrs. Avery hospital bills. The word got out and it was done at all the shows. The city of Cincinnati wants all of you to know they care. Mrs. Avery and the unborn child are in their prayers. Also, that the drunk driver will not get away with it. We all intend to see to it."

Hoss accepts it with tears in his eyes. "Tell everyone thank you from all of us. This will be a huge help."

When Hoss arrives at the hospital the next morning, he takes T. J aside to talk things over. "Hey big brother. Has there been any change since we left?"

"Not much except we know now that she does know part of what's going on. As they bathed her late last night, she groaned as if something was hurting her. Other than that there hasn't been anything else."

"That's good news. It means she is still in there and is fighting for her and the baby's life. Now T. J I have some other news. First the audience took up collection for her medical bills. I acceptedit and gave it to the billing department on my way up. Before you even say anything, we didn't do this. I was surprised when security took me aside and gave me the money."

"Okay Hoss. Now I have questions for you. Have you guys packed up to move yet?"

"Not yet. The manager says we can stay put for a while if need be."

"Okay butat what cost to us?"

"He said not to worry about it. There will be no charge. He also said Sabrina has done a lot for him, the stadium and his family."

"Yes it was a long time ago but he owes her that much."

"T. J he says he put Sabrina on the prayer warriors list at his church."

"That's great Hoss. She needs all the prayers she can get.

Now onto rodeo business. I think we should take him up on the offer. We will reschedule with Dayton arena. Then we will go onto Cleveland straight out of Cincinnati. That should give her time to recover. Now let's call the arena Also,this will give the animals a chance to rest up a bit."

"T. J, what if Cleveland comes before Sabrina wakes up?"

"Well Hoss we will cross that bridge when we get to it. For now I think we all need to worry about being here for Sabrina. I think she will need to see our smiling faces when she wakes up. That will be our way of letting her know we love her."

"You know big brother, I do believe you are right again."

## CHAPTER 16

It has been almost a week since Sabrina was in the wreck. There has been little change in Sabrina. She has shown that she knows when her loved ones are in the room. T. J has barely left her side. As he sits with her he reads a book to her. At night he quietly plays flute music for her. Now Monica walks in the room. "Hello T. J how is our favorite patient? Has the doctor been in yet to update us?"

"No Monica he hasn't yet. So far I have found a little bit at a time. She's trying to come back to us."

"T. J you need to go get a shower and get some rest. I will stay with Sabrina until you get back."

"Monica I really don't want to leave her. I want to be with her when she wakes up."

"I promise if she even sneezes I will let you know."

"Okay I can take a hint. You should at least talk to her or even read while I am gone."

"Trust me I will. I may even sing softly now get."

"Yes Momma!" Monica settles in as T. J headed to shower and grabbed a bite to eat.

It is now 2a.m and T. J has went to sleep in the chair next to Sabrina's bed. Sabrina opened her eyes to see him sitting there sleeping. The nurse walks in. Sabrina motions for her to let him sleep. Skylar, her nurse whispers "Welcome back Sabrina."

"How long have I been out?"

"Almost a week."

"How is my baby?"

"Doing well. The doctor wanted to take the baby but T. J wouldn't let him. He said that's not what either of you would want."

"He is so right."

"That's not all he fired that doctor. He brought in one that your mom said you used to always see."

"Good job Mom."

"Okay I will leave you alone to rest now. You will have another nurse in a few hours."

"Thank you."

"You're welcome now just rest."

"I will."

It is 6:30a.m and Sabrina opened her eyes again. T. J was still asleep but resting his head on the bed. She puts her hand gently on his head and stroked his long blonde hair. He looked up to see her smiling down at him. "Good morning, beautiful."

"Good morning,sweetheart. How long have you been awake? How are you feeling? Can you feel the baby move?"

"Stop T. J. One question at a time. First,long have I been awake? What time? The first time was between 2 and 3. Then, there was this last time. Well, only a few minutes when you woke up to my hand in your hair. Next question, how do I feel? Well, like I have been hit head-on by a bus. Last, can I feel the baby move? Well, just a little no more or less than before."

"Hey you! The nurse said you are back with us!"

"Well, Doc as you can see I am."

"Yes I definitely see that. T. J, would you mind leaving while I get a few nurses in here to help me examine her?"

"Yeah sure. I need to grab some coffee and a bite to eat. Is she on a special diet?"

"No, not that I ordered."

"Good! I'll bring you a bite as well."

"Thank you baby."

"You're welcome"

"I will be back in a little while."

"See you then."

"Okay now that he is out of here, drop the act. I know you oh to well. What are you hiding?"

"Tell the nurses not to let anyone in, until you say otherwise."

"Done. Now get it all out."

"Doc I am scared. I can't feel anything from the waist down. Also, I lied to T. J- something I said I would never do. I told him I could still feel the baby, Doc. I can't. Is my baby okay? Probably, the baby was fine as of 9 o'clock last night. Please check for me."

"Okay. Then relax, so I can."

"Yeah okay, that's good."

"Yes. Now that I felt it, the baby is doing great. What a relief! Thank you."

"You are more than welcome. Okay now I will order some test so we can figure out what's going on."

"Good. That works.'

"Okay I will go set up the test."

"Thank you."

"Now we will get some answers."

The tests have been run and T. J brought Sabrina back a sandwich and fries. She was eating as T. J tells her how things are with the rodeo. "Sabrina, why didn't you tell me about the baby as soon as you found out?"

"T. J I tried to talk to you but you never had time to listen. Then when I tried the last time, you went to sleep. I don't even know for sure what you heard so I left. Next thing I knew, a vehicle was headed right at me."

"Sabrina, everyone knows you were involved in a bad wreck."

"Okay I get it. I will just shut up. You really don't want to know or care what went on after impact. I get it by the way don't you have a rodeo to run somewhere? "Sabrina, that's not fair."

"Don't tell me about fair."

The doctor comes in he has the charge nurse with him. "Sabrina, I am going to have the nurse help me with running new I. V's. Also I will be putting you on some new meds through your I. V line. T. J, can you please excuse us for a few? Give us about ten minutes. Looks like her new bed has arrived we will need to move her over to it."

"Sure. I will be back after I make some phone calls."

"Thank you."

"Okay Doctor Brown, he's gone. Okay spill it. What is wrong?"

"There is no way to say this except that you have some spinal damage that may never heal. You could end up permanently paralyzed. Let's pray that's not the case. I have ordered for you to have massage therapy three times a day. We will see how that goes."

"Thanks doc."

T. J comes back in the room long after the doctor has left. Sabrina has nodded off but opens her eyes when he comes over by her. "Sorry did I wake you?"

"No not really."

"Sabrina, you may have been right. If Hoss doesn't clear things up, I may have to go sort things out in Cleveland."

"Just go T. J I know you don't really want to be here anyway. My mom will be back tomorrow morning anyway."

"Sabrina, you know that's not so. I said 'if' that is a big word for two little letters. You are terribly wrong. I would rather be here with you. Are you mad at me again?"

"No. Just hurt but that too will end."

# CHAPTER 17

It has been almost a week since T. J left because Hoss couldn't sign things that needed signing. Monica has been spending a lot of time with Sabrina while the kids are in preschool. Sabrina still hasn't told her mom Monica what is going on yet. She has high hopes that everything will turn around. She will get the feeling back. So far her hopes and prayers haven't worked. Sabrina decides that it's time. She needs to tell her Mom what is going on.

"Good Morning Breezy."

"Good Morning Mom."

"Mom, I have a few things I need to tell you."

"Okay baby but, this doesn't sound too positive."

"Well, Mom I'm not sure yet. Please hear me out before you say anything."

"Okay Sabrina go ahead. I am listening."

"Well. Mom you see there was more damage than I let the doctor tell all of you."

"How much kiddo?"

"Well, let me finish. There is spinal damage but bottomline the baby is fine. Me on the other hand? Well, I can't feel anything from the waist down. Yes, Mom I am paralyzed. Will I get the feeling back? Who knows? So I decided to give it to God. If I am supposed to ever walk again, only time will tell. Please don't pity or baby me. I have to deal with it in my own way."

"Okay Breezy I won't but I have a question? Now that you told me, when do you get out of here?"

"This afternoon. I have already hired a full -time nurse."
"Good. You will need one."

It is now 3 in the afternoon and the doctor is with Sabrina and Monica. "Okay Sabrina. Firstyour electric wheelchair will arrive at the farm in the morning. Next, we want to thank you for hiring Skylar full- time. She was only able to get part- time hours here. Skylar will be arriving at your place either this evening or first thing tomorrow."

"I know, doc. We already made the arrangements."

"Lastly, whatever you do, don't forget your therapy at home and don't miss appointments here either."

"I won't. I want to hopefully walk again and maybe even ride my horses again." "Sabrina, I won't lie to you. I never have. You may be looking at major spinal surgery in the future."

"I kind of figured that. Let's see what happens."

Now settled in at the farm, Skylar has been set up in the small guest house just off the main house. Sabrina's bathroom has been handicapped equipped. The kids seem to be taking it in stride. They are just glad to have their Mom back home with them. T. J still hasn't called nor does he know what is going on. It seems as though he left the hospital and forgot about Sabrina again. Sabrina is not in the least surprised by his lack of communication. Monica on the other hand plans to call T. J tonight after everyone has gone to bed. She knows that will make Sabrina a bit mad but she doesn't really care. She did tell T. J she would keep him updated daily. So far she has kept her word to him, now is no different. She thinks he needs to know she has left the hospital at the least.

"Mom where are my little darling children?"

"Oh hello dear. They are out in the barn showing off the animals to Skylar. Stop there Breezy! They are fine. I already warned them not to get her hurt. Plus, I told her not to go in with the bull. Diablo is not as mean as you think especially with women."

"I guess you're right though mom. By the way how is he doing? According to the vet he is a 100% again. I just haven't said anything to Jeremy. He doesn't want his Dad to put his baby on the circuit. Do you blame him mom? He doesn't want to chance Lance or anyone being mean to him again."

"No, I guess not Breezy but you know he will eventually end up going to the rodeo."

"Maybe. But let's not worry about that right now."

"Okay. We won't."

Now that everyone has had dinner and is settled in for the night, Sabrina wheels in to hear her Mom on the phone with T. J. "Mom you betrayed me, didn't you?"

"No, Sabrina I did not."

"Yes, you did. I heard you talking to T. J. If he cared that much about me, he would have called me. I have not heard from him since he left. I have had enough. He does care about you he has been calling me every night to check on things."

"See?You just said it yourself calling you. Well, if you want him he's all yours. I can't even be a real woman to him anymore anyway. GOODNIGHT!"

The next morning Sabrina does not come in for breakfast. Jeremy goes to check on her. "Morning Mom!"

"Morning buddy."

"Mom, how come you didn't eat breakfast?"

"I am just not very hungry this morning. I will eat in a little while. Jeremy, I am thinking about having Uncle Hoss come get you and the twins along with the animals and take you to be with your dad at the rodeo."

"Mom, I don't want to go with Dad. I want for me and Diablo to stay here with you."

"Son, you knew Diablo would have to go when he healed. Plus, you guys need to spend time with your Dad."

"But Mommy that's not fair."

"Yes it is. Plus, you will be with him. That's final you are going."

## CHAPTER 18

"Sabrina, what the hell do you think you are doing?! Jeremy came to me in tears. You are mad at me and I won't have you taking it out on the children!"

"Let's get something straight. They are my children. I gave birth to them not you. Therefore, Monica I will do what I feel is in their best interest. Besides no one said you couldn't go with them. They are going that's final."

"You are definitely just like your father stubborn! Go ahead storm out then."

"Look who's talking!"

Hoss shows up and loads the animals. He doesn't take Mara or WaKeya Sabrina wanted them left behind. T. J is walking the floor when Hoss gets back. He proceeds to jump Hoss when he gets out of the truck before he even knows where he went. "Hey Daddy!" the twins call out as they run and wrap their arms around him.

"Wow! Well hello, you two."

"Uncle Hoss says we get to ride in the shows."

"Yes and I will see to it. Now get your ponies and go find J. C. He will help you settle them in."

"Okay Daddy."

"Now Hoss, where is Sabrina?"

"She didn't come."

"What do you mean she didn't come?"

"She left instructions for me with Monica. I was to pick them up with all the animals but her two horses."

"He's right. Sorry T. J. She isn't coming."

"Mom Monica what do you mean?"

"Well, I managed to piss her off and so did you. She hadn't heard from you since you came back to the rodeo. She made the comment that she was right. nothing changed. You didn't want to be with her anyway."

"Damn! I hate it when she is right."

"She is though. She also said other things that I won't even bring up. You can probably guess though because you have checked with me. You called me every day buthaven't called her even once."

"Again, she is right. I guess I will have to go settle this myself. She wants to be a pompous ass so can I!" T. J storms off before Monica can say anything to him.

T. J is in his truck headed for Cincinnati. He has tried several times to call but she doesn't answer. He gets madder by the mile. It is now six in the evening as he pulls into the driveway at the farm. Skylar has just settled Sabrina in her room. She had dinner, a shower and is watching a movie. T. J pulls up and shuts down the engine. He walks up to the door, Skylar opens the door right away. "Well, hello. You must be T. J?"

"Yes. And you are? I am Sabrina's full-time nurse."

"What are you talking about?"

"Well, she hired me to take care of her while she heals the rest of the way. Sit have some tea so we can talk."

"Okay. I think I will."

"I am guessing you weren't told? Sabrina still has a lot of rehab to do and maybe some major surgery."

"No and what do you mean? What's wrong with her she seemed fine when I left?"

"Oh! She must have kept a lot from you."

"Yes obviously. Now,will you please fill me in?"

"I guess this may be my job but okay I will."

"No, it won't. If she tries to fire you, I will see to it she doesn't. That's a guarantee."

"Here goes. Sabrina is paralyzed from the waist down. If she doesn't get any better she may be looking at major spinal surgery."

"Oh my god! No. I was not told. You mean she can't walk? She can't get out of bed or even use the bathroom by herself?"

"No T. J. I am afraid not."

"Why would she keep this from me? She doesn't feel like she is a whole woman as she puts it."

"Bullshit! That's a cop out, isn't it?"

"She is afraid she won't even know when her labor starts. I personally think she is more scared than anything."

"Sabrina scared? That's a crock! She's never been afraid of anything."

"Okay. You will have to see for yourself. She is in the main bedroom. Tell you what let's wait till morning."

"I will settle in the living room on thecouch. I want to be the one to help her in the morning."

"Okay if that's what you want."

The next morning Sabrina screamed out for Skylar. She has fallen trying to get in the wheelchair. T. J is up in a flash almost knocking Skylar down to get to Sabrina. He runs in and sees her on the floor. Worried he goes to her and starts to pick her up. Skylar stops him. "T. J you can't just pick her up. I need to make sure she's okay and the baby is as well." Skylar gets down on the floor with Sabrina and starts taking her vitals. Next, she listens to the baby's heart beat. "T. J would you like to hear this? It's the baby's heart beat."

"Yes I would."

"Hey, you two! Don't I have a say in this? The baby is in my belly. "Yes. Do you want to hear ittoo?"

"Not yet. Let T. J go first."

"Wow! It sounds like a lot of drums beating in there."

"What are you talking about?" Sabrina takes the stethoscope away from T. J and listens for herself. "He's right. Skylar, something isn't right." Skylar takes a listen as well. She looks up and says,"The last time I heard something like that was a woman carrying more than one child."

"Oh dear! God not again! T. J If I am carrying twins again, you're getting fixed. Better yet I will. If I have no insides, I can't get pregnant again. Now can someone please get me off this floor? It's making my back hurt."

T. J gently picks her up and puts her on the bed.
"T. J do that again."
"Do what again?"
"The way you moved my legs, do it again."
"Oh good god. I feel some of the pressure! This must mean I may get some feeling back in the part of my body that quit me."
"I am praying you do. I would hate to be outrun by a wheelchair."
"Very funnysmartass."
"It would be pretty cool though to be able to say my wife drives better than me even in a wheelchair."
"Okay T. J enough with the wheelchair cracks. Sabrina, I just set up an appointment for you to go have an ultrasound and sonogram. It will be at 2:00p.m today at U. C's medical building."
"Good! I will take her. I hope so. I told them we would be with her."
"Smart thinking, Sky. I knew I liked you for some reason."

# CHAPTER 19

At U. C, SABRINA, TJ and Skylar are waiting for the test results and the doctors to read them as well.

"T. J something must be terribly wrong. They hardly ever call the doctor to come in as well to read the results on screen."

"Calm down, babe. I am sure with all you've been through they just want another opinion."

"No T. J. That's not it. Something is wrong."

"Here comes the doctor. He will tell us soon."

"Hello. I know we have never met but I am Doctor Fitzpatrick. I will be checking the monitor to see what we have going on in there. Well, I see what nurse Skylar was talking about. I am to understand you already have a set of twins?"

"Yes that would be correct."

"Also, I have been informed of you being in a bad car accident."

"Correct again."

"Here let me help you sit up."

"Doc, you don't understand. She's paralyzed from the waist down."

"Sir I do understand and I know that. I do believe with everything that has happened, part of her having no feeling also comes from her pregnancy as well. Her body is trying to protect these babies."

"Babies? What do you mean babies?"

"Mrs. Avery, how far along are you?"

"Between 5 and 6 months."

"Why do you ask?"

"That's about right then. You see any pregnant woman in a crash as bad as you were , the baby would not have made it. But these three maybe four have. Yeah I know that look says it all. You wasn't expecting tohear that twins, yes. triplets or quads, no. I get it. But it's true. Hope you two are ready for this."

"Not on your life. We weren't even planning anymore yet."

"Well, guess you will have a full-sized family all at once."

"We already have a big family. Well, we only have three at the present time but we own a ranch and everyone there is our family as well."

"I will let you two talk. I will come back in a bit. You can help her get dressed."

"T. J what are we going to do? We have the rodeo going on. We have to see it through. Plus, everything else that's on our plate. We can't do this!"

"We can, we will and we are. Sabrina, I love you with everything that I am. I couldn't stand to be without you. I don't want anyone else. You and the kids are my world." "Sweetheart,about the comment you made earlier- you are right. I will call Hoss and have him and Mom come down to the farm."

"Yes after the events are over in Cleveland. They can come as soon as the animals are in Dayton."

"Why are you calling Hoss and Mom?"

"Because, we need them to oversee things on the circuit for a while. I want to be with you."

"What about the kids?"

"That is why I am having Mom come too. I am going to let her drive my pickup and help at the rodeo with the kids. I will go buy us a small car to drive to appointments and so on. Also I am going to get myself fixed. You don't have to, I can instead." "No I want to. I think between us we will have enough on our plates just raising the ones we have." "Yeah. You're right about that."

"So do we agree?"

"Yes. We will both get fixed."

"Hey we can still have fun pretending."

"You're bad Breezy but that's another reason I love you so much."

Now back at the farm, T. J has helped Skylar get Sabrina set up in the living room. She was complaining about being cooped up in the bedroom. "Thank you T. J. I think this is too much on you. Are you sure you want to do this?"

"Do what? Take care of my wife and unborn children. Absolutely! You and my children are my world. So don't go getting hormonal on me now. Just do as the doctor says and relax. Skylar and I have things covered."

"I love you. Now, I have to go get us a car."

"Better make it a mini van. Sounds like we will need it."

"Yeah maybe you're right butwe will see."

"Okay T. J. I Love you!"

## CHAPTER 20

A few days later T. J and Sabrina are in at the kitchen table when everyone shows up. They knock on the door and Skylar opened it. She opens it to see a giant of a man standing in front of her. "Hello you must be Skylar? Well I am Hoss, T. J's younger brother."

"Well, all of you should come on in. T. J and Sabrina are at the table."

"Thank you ma'am!"

"You are more than welcome!" The whole crew files in. They introduce themselves as they do. Skylar is amazed to see how many people care and love Sabrina.

"Hey! What are all of you doing here?"

"T. J said you two wanted to see us as soon as the Dayton show was set up so here we are. Now what can we do to help?"

"Well, first let me start by saying thank you all for coming. Then, I think we should share the news in person."

"Okay but what news could that be that you couldn't tell us by phone."

"Hush, Hoss. Let him talk."

"Now what's up, you two?"

"Thanks Monica! Well here goes. Monica we will need you to travel with the rodeo. We want you to take care of the kids as they travel with the show. Then, we will need for all of you to take care of running the rodeo until Sabrina is ready to come back.

Now for the other news-the reason we wanted to tell you in person. Here goes. As you all may know, Sabrina suffered some very horrific injuries in the accident. It left her paralyzed from the waist down among other things. Well, it seems as though those injuries were also due to her pregnancy. Yes, you all heard me. She is pregnant. Now from all of that, her body steps in to protect the babies. Now wait we said the same thing. The good news is, she may possibly regain the feeling after the birth.

With all of that is going on, I plan to stay here and take care of Sabrina."

"Okay T. J now can we speak?"

"Yes Hoss. What's on your mind?"

"First, congratulations are in order. Then I am guessing twins again because you said babies."

"No, Hoss. We are having triplets or quads."

"Come on, Sabrina. Quit pulling our chain."

"No I am serious. I was not expecting to even be pregnantand to find this out was a shock to T. J and I. So to answer the question, we are having more than one."

"Okay. Sorry Breezy I was just asking."

"T. J I told you this is more than anyone can deal with. I will be in my room."

"Did I say something wrong?"

"No Hoss. She's just not dealing well right now. She seems to think she is a burden to us. There is no guarantee that she will ever walk again. Lunch is here. Enjoy. I am going in with Sabrina for a while."

"Doesn't she know she would never be a burden to any of us?"

"No Hoss. I guess she doesn't."

"You need to understand my daughter has never depended on anyone. Sabrina has always been the one to step up and help others not the other way around. That's just how she has been her whole life. Hopefully T. J can get her to eat something."

"Should I take her something?"

"No Hoss. That would make it worse. I will set aside a r a plate for her. She will eat when she settles down a bit."

"Okay mom. You know her best. I guess we should go eat?"

"Yeah. I think you're right."

"Sabrina, please talk to me."

"T. J, I don't know what you could expect from me. Here I am a crippled pregnant woman carrying triplets at the least. Hell, I am worse than a dog. I can't even produce enough tits or milk for my babies."

"Wow! what a slut puppy."

"Sorry T. J I just call it as I see it. So you see I really don't know what else there is to say."

"Well then I guess that makes me a male horror. I mean those are my babies you are pregnant with. So I guess we are in a big dilemma aren't we? If you are a burden then so am I. So where do we go from here?"

T. J walks over to her to find she is crying. "Sabrina, I know things won't be easy. Baby please don't cry I can't stand to see you cry."

"T. J, it's not the money this time. Moreover, it's the fact that I can't help take care of these babies. Well it's just just not right to put them off on everyone else. Hell, we still have three older children also. Really 6 or 7 would be a bit much without my help."

"Stop thinking that way Sabrina. We will get through this. Besides. everyone already loves our other three. What's not to love? They look like my beautiful wife. So now babe, let's get something to eat. Besides we can't let those babies do without a meal. Oh yeah and you probably need to eat also."

"Oh T. J now you're teasing me."

"I know but at least you are smiling. Now let's go eat."

"Hey Sabrina! I'm sorry if I upset you. I hope you are okay? Here let me get you a plate. What would you like?"

"How about I go with you to get it?"

"Okay that works. Don't worry about anything at the rodeo we got it."

"Believe me, I know everything is in good hands there. I can't wait for these precious little ones to come."

"Seeing how I am Uncle Hoss, I will get to help with them. I plan to spoil them the same way I do the other three."
"Good god help us!"
"No, that's my job to help."
"Hoss, behave before I throw something at you."
"Yes ma'am."
"Don't ma'am, me!"
"Okay Sis!"

# CHAPTER 21

It has been almost two months since everyone moved on with the rodeo. The quads were born a week ago. Sabrina woke up and noticed that T. J was not in the room. She thought to herself that the babies must have woken him. She decided to try and get out of bed herself to go to the bathroom. This is when she realized she has moved her legs without any help. She is so excited she now knows she will walk again. So she managed to stand holding on to the side of the bed. Slowly, she got to the wheelchair. Sabrina felt a little weak but planned to continue working on it. She rolled herself into the bathroom and did what she needed to do then headed to the kitchen.

"Good morning Skylar."

"How did you get in here by yourself?"

"Well, that's kind of another story. What did you do? Never mind don't answer that I don't think I want to know."

"Okay if you say so. I could really use a cup of coffeeand maybe a little breakfast."

"Okay. I will get it for you."

"Thank you. Now I think while you are doing that I should tell you. I woke up and sat up wondering where T. J was. I saw the time so I figured the both of you were tending to our little miracles. So I decided to try and get out of bed myself. That's when I noticed I could move my legs on my own. So I used the bed to stand and work my way to the wheelchair. It felt so great to be able to do that for myself. I am still weak but I plan to keep working on getting stronger. So now you know how I managed to get in here on my own."

"Does this mean you won't be needing me here real soon?"

"No it doesn't mean that at all. I was thinking about seeing if you would be willing to travel with us? Of course it would come with extra benefits. Like besides your pay, all other expenses like travel living, food et cetera will be taken care of."

"Why would you do that and are you sure?"

"Well, our extended family could use a good nurse. Plus, we could use help with the kids so I am positive. Think about it and let me know."

"What if I said yes with one other thing?"

"What other thing is that?"

"I want to learn to ride a horse."

"Oh! I forgot to tell you everyone has to be able to handle and ride our horses." "Then I don't need to think about it I accept gladly."

"Good! Then, that's settled."

"Honey, I was looking for you."

"Well here I am."

"Babe, I don't want to leave you at all but I need to go to Milwaukee. Hoss needs someone to look at a few animals to add to the circuit."

"Then, we will all go."

"Babe are you sure? If something happens I may not be close enough to protect you."

"Sabrina, maybe you should tell him?"

"How about I show him?"

"Show me what? Sabrina!"

"T. J don't. I got this you need to see what I learned this morning."

"Oh my god! it's a miracle you're standing."

"Yes and with work, I will be walking again soon.

Babe you go ahead of us. You fly in. Skylar and I will take care of a few things here then we will join you."

"Okay. Are you sure you got this?"

"Of course. I do have the best help there is next to you. Skylar can help me and handle things with the babies. Look, here is a straight through flight that leaves at 4p.m. It puts you in there at 4:45."

"Okay, book it. I will see if David or his wife can come take you to the airport." "That would be great as long as it doesn't put them out. T. J they won't do it if they have other things going on. How about we just Uber a ride?"

"Yeah, there's a good idea. Now that's done I can spend some time with the little babies before I have to leave."

"Okay. You do that then."

"Skylar, have you ever flown anywhere before?"

"No, Ma'am."

"What's wrong?"

"I never been anywhere but here, Kentucky and

"Well, I guess you are in for a real treat then. We travel all over the country. This small farm belongs to me. Then we have a 2000 plus acre ranch in Texas. I lived here all my life until I came into some money. I bought the ranch and not long after that I fell for T. J and married him. The ranch came with all the staff that was left after it started going downhill. I stepped in and thanks to Hoss ,bought it. We put it back to its full glory and then some. You will learn more about it as time goesby."

"Hey babe. The driver is here to pick me up."

"Okay. Wow, what a kiss!"

"I will never leave you again or go to bed without kissing you first. I love you babe!"

"I love you too. Be careful. Please don't buy until you know what we are getting."

"I won't. If we buy they will all need shots et cetera…so they can travel with us."

"Glad I taught you something."

"Oh, Sabrina stop teasing! One more kiss then I have to go. See you there tomorrow."

"See you then."

"Sabrina, where did you come up with the names for the little ones?"

"Well, we already have Jeremy he's the oldest. He's 8yrs old. Then, we have the two twins Matthew and Amanda. So we named these four after T. J and other family members. First we have Tommy and Tammy after T. J. Then there is Terry after Teresa. Last, is Tony after his uncle Hoss. Hoss doesn't know I know his middle name is Tony." Now you know where the names came from."

"You mean there are only two girls out of seven kids?"

"Yes I am afraid so."

The next morning Sabrina loaded Wakeya And Mara on a horse transport with the help of the driver. Next, she sent the van on loaded with all the extra stuff needing to go on. Now, she and Skylar are at the airport with the fourbabies. They have chartered a private plane out. Sabrina wanted the babies and Skylar to be comfortable. They are in the plane waiting to be cleared for take-off. The babies are fastened and buckled in their car seats.

Skylar look at Tommy. He is all smiles. He's the only one awake. "I think he takes after his Dad. T. J can't sleep unless his in a bed lying down. Tammy must have taken after me. She closes her eyes and she's asleep. Then Tony and Terry must take after their Grandpa Sanders."

"Who's is that?"

"My Daddy. He would get up early and be up all day. Then at bedtime or when he traveled, he would sleep. I still miss him so much. Skylar, do you believe in life after death?"

"Yeah I would like to think there is. Why do you ask?"

"You know I died during the wreck. Well, there is life after death. I got to see my Dad and my Grandma. It was so beautiful there. I was told it wasn't my time yet. I would have to come back. So I asked to just get a little more time with them. I was allowed just a bit longer."

"Everyone, please make sure your seat belts are fastened. We are clear for take-off. We will be arriving in Milwaukee at about 11a.m eastern time. The skies are clear and we looking forward to an easy flight. A stewardess will be in to check on you as soon as we are in the air. Thank you and have an enjoyable flight. This is Captain Johnson out."

"Sabrina, did you get to share this with T. J?"

"Do you mean about what I witnessed from the other side? No I didn't want to upset him. He too was in a bad shape right after we started to get the ranch back in order. He was in a bad roll over. A steer tire blew on the new truck I bought him. We were headed home from purchasing some Livestock. I watched it blow and then roll. I sure thought he was gone. We did lose a few cattle and he had to be airlifted. I found out that same night I couldn't give blood because I was pregnant with the twins. We will talk about it later just not right now."

"I can see you two have been through a lot together."

"You can say that again."

"Sabrina, do you think that I will find someone like that?"

"I don't know, honey. There is no reason why you couldn't. You are a very pretty young lady."

"Yeah, but, I am scared because I am still a virgin and the last guy dumped me. I wouldn't have sex with him because I want to save it for my wedding night."

"Stick to your guns on that. If the guy truly loves you, he will understand and be willing to wait."

"I hope you are right. T. J and I waited. So you see a good guy will wait.

Hey do me a favor? Don't fall for any of these guys at the rodeo without asking me about them first. There are a few losers riding the rodeo circuit. Just for starters, Lance and the crew he hangs with. They think they are god's gift to bull riding, roping and especially women. I have already had run-ins with them. We don't talk about it because it hurts T. J too much. It is believed that Lance had something to do with Cathy's death. Cathy was T. J's fiancée. She was in the arena before a show when a very mean bull got out and came at her and her horse. She went down before T. J could get to them. She took a horn to the heart. Until he met me, he didn't want any part of women or rodeo's again. So please don't mention it."

"I won't. Thanks for the heads up though."

"You're Welcome."

"This is your Captain speaking. We are approaching Milwaukee airport now. So again please fasten your seat belts. Hope you had a wonderful flight. Thank you for chartering Small Air Cincinnati."

# CHAPTER 22

Sabrina had set it up for the hotel to pick them up. The hotel van was waiting when they landed. Now with the children settled in and fed, Sabrina calls the arena. A woman answered and she asked for T. J. The response was that T. J was too busy to take any calls from lovesick fans. Sabrina hung up a little pissed then thought to herself she knew better. Why didn't she just call his cell?

T. J's cell rang then went to voice mail. "T. J, this is a lovesick fan and your wife," she says on a message as she laughs. "Please call me. We are settled at the Hilton Hotel." She hung up.

"Sabrina are you okay? Oh you're laughing."

"Yes I am okay and yes I am laughing."

"How are the angels accepting their surroundings?"

"They have fullbellies, dry butts,and are fastasleep."

"God lord! Didin't they get enough sleep on the plane?!"

"Yeah but you of all people should know babies like their sleep after they eat."

"Yeah. So true!"

Sabrina's cell phone rang. It was Hoss. "Hey what's going on?"

"Your horses and van just arrived."

"Yes I sent them. Where is your brother?"

"Last I saw him he was headed to pick up somelivestock."

"You mean he didn't tell you?"

"Tell me what?"

"We thought maybe my mom, Monica would want to ride them and compete. Plus, he said you guys needed another van for the crew."

"Quit pulling my leg. The van, I can see that. On the other hand, you don't let anyone ride WaKeya but, you!"

"You better think again. Mom helped raise him."

"Oh, sorry. I will keep an eye on them for you then."

"I was counting on it. Just bed them down good and give them plenty of hay. They already had breakfast. Talk to you soon." Sabrina hangs up then laughs so hard she almost falls over.

"Sabrina that was cruel."

"No, it wasn't. He's gullible. He'll fall for just about anything. Besides if T. J wanted them to know, he would have told them. I messaged mom and let her in on it. She thinks it's funny so she will add to it as well. You'll see. If I know mom, she will be here in a little while. Besides she hasn't met her grandbabies yet. You think we're bad? When Mom sees them, she will spoil them. Hell, the whole crew will. On a good note, they will not want for a clean diaper or to be fed. They will also be well taken care of."

"Okay. You must know what you are doing."

"Trust me I do."

A few hours later T. J and Monica show up at the Hotel. T. J walked in, went over to Sabrina and gave her a big kiss. "Well, hello handsome! Hi Mom. What did you finally tell Hoss?"

"We kept up the story you told him. He's having a fit."

"Oh, well let him have his little fit. I can't wait to see the look on his face when I show up."

"What are you up to, Sabrina?"

"Me up to something? No, not me."

"Sabrina, I know you better than that. Whatever it is, just don't get yourself hurt."

"I won't. We just want to surprise everyone."

"Okay then. Now where are those precious little angels of ours?"

"There in here, Mrs. Sanders."

"Just call me Mom or Grandma. Everyone else does."

"Okay, if that's what you wish."

"Yes. That's what I wish. How long have they been asleep?"

"Well, it is time for them to wake up. Go ahead, I know you want to."

"Wow! He has beautiful eyes."

"They all do. That's Tommy. Go ahead pick him up."

"T. J, what are you doing?"

"Waking Tony up. Hello, little man. Come to Daddy. Skylar, yes. Will you hand me Tammy?"

"Sure. Then I will get Terry. Hey mommy's little princess. Time you open them eyes I know you are awake."

"They are all so precious."

"I was hoping you would think that."

"How can I not? They are my grandbabies."

"Mom, there will be no more after these four. T. J took care of it. Plus because of the wreck, they had to do a full hysterectomy on me. We had to put them onSymilac. I didn't produce enough milk for even just one. The good news is it was all done vaginally. Therefore, I don't have to worry about stitches."

"Sabrina, the seven we have are more than enough."

"I thought you might see it that way. T. J, how do you feel about it?"

"Hell, I am glad this is it. I don't want to take a chance on losing her. Besides I was beginning to think if I just looked at Sabrina she would get pregnant."

"Real funny, T. J. There is five years between them and the twins. Were you trying to get pregnant?"

"God, no! I wanted to at least wait until the rodeo season was over."

"Okay. I see your point."

"Well now that the babies are settled again, Mom you need to get back with their dinner."

"Yeah, true. I will be along shortly."

"Okay. See you there. Mom, wait here's my credit card. Get some pizza andchicken. That should make everyone happy."

"What about you?"

"I will grab something on my way back."

"Okay. See you there."

"Don't forget ring time starts tonight at 7:00p.m."

"How could I forget? I'm riding tonight."

"Okay. See you there."

"Skylar, in a little bit we will get the babies dressed."

"For what?"

"We are all going to the arena tonight. T. J will be doing the opening ceremony. He will introduce the babies to everyone during the opening. He will have some of our more experienced riders come into the arena with him."

"Is this safe?"

"Yes or we wouldn't do it. Matthew and Amanda were introduced this way as well. The difference is that it was at a local rodeo back home. It will be Hoss, Jose, J. C and Teresa. You will hand them to each rider as they enter the arena."

"Okay. I guess you know what's best."

"T. J will already be on his horse in the arena doing the announcements."

"Where will you be?"

"Close by. You'll see."

"Okay!"

# CHAPTER 23

At the arena, T. J has mounted up and is headed in the arena (? Perhaps, ring?). Meanwhile T. J has the chosen four standing outside thein gate. Skylar walks up and says, "Hello. As I call your name reach down and take the front strap." Confused they agree. She then hands the babies off to their uncles and aunt. Skylar is confused yet again because Sabrina has disappeared. Confused but doing as she was asked. she stays close to the in gate. "Okay everyone. They have all been fed and have dry bottoms. They should all be very satisfied andhappy. Just please be careful with those preciousangels.".
"
"We will," Hoss replied smiling.

"Good Evening ladies and gentlemen. Welcome to the rodeo! I thought we might start by saying you have probably heard we almost lost one of our cowgirls. She was in a very bad wreck in Cincinnati during one of our earlier events. That's when we learned that she was pregnant. So I thought we might start off by saying though lots of prayer and miracles, she survived. Yes, it was a close call. She was met head-on by a semi going the wrong way on the interstate. Not only did she survive, so did the four precious little angels she was carrying.

We would to start off by introducing those precious little Angels. Coming into the arena is Hoss carrying his namesake, Tony. Next is Teresa carrying her namesake, Terry. Then, carrying my namesake, Tommy is Jose. Last but not least is J. C carrying Tammy. Let's give these little future cowboys and cowgirl a warmwelcome." The crowd claps and cheers. "Now if any of you are wondering why they are named after us. Well, because these are the last four of our seven.

Okay, sorry ladies but yes I am spoken for. I am married to the beautiful Sabrina Avery. Now may I introduce to you Matthew and Amanda, our twins, riding their ponies. They are 5 years old. They love showing everyone that little doesn't mean they can't ride with the big guys. Coming into the arena is our 8 year old Jeremy. Wait a minute. Does your mom know you are on her mustang, Mara."

"Yes, Daddy she told me to."

"Okay if you say so. I wouldn't want to be you if she doesn't know about this." "She knows. I wouldn't want to her (?) when you see her."

"What on earth are two up to?"

"You'll see!"

"Come guys! We gotta let the riders come in for the national anthem."

"Okay, Bubby. Let's go."

"I think that means you all can leave as well."

Everyone filed out one by one. The national anthem began. Sabrina walked in on WaKeyA carrying the American flag. She took her place next to T. J in the center of the ring. The rest of the riders came in carrying a flag of Wisconsin, the rodeo circuit, and flags representing each branch of the military. T. J turns his microphone off. "Sabrina, are you sure you should be doing this?"

"Yes, I figure this is a good start. I got some feeling back in my legs yesterday. I wanted to surprise you. I am not 100% yet but at least I can do this. You may need to help me down though."

"Gladly."

The music stopped, T. J turned his microphone back on, "Ladies and gentlemen-my wife, Sabrina. Up until now I didn't know she was getting feeling back in her legs. Sabrina, would you to lead us in prayer?"

"Yes I would. Dear Lord, we come to you tonight in prayer. We don't ask for the best time, highest score or even the perfect ride; We just ask that you keep us safe until you call us home to that beautiful arena in the sky-where we finally hear your voice saying,'Welcome home cowboy or cowgirl. Your dues and entry fee has already been paid', We also ask that you safely see our patrons and their love ones home after the event tonight. Lastly, we ask that you let them enjoy their time at the rodeo. Amen. Thank You everyone and hope you enjoy the show."

Now back by the stalls T. J reached up and helped Sabrina off her horse. "T. J don't let go. I can't stand by myself without something to hold onto yet. My legs are stillweak."

"Then why did you ride your horse?"

"Because I trust him. Plus,it will help strengthen my legs. Watch. Let me use your arm to help get me to my chair."

"Okay just take it slow."

"I will trust me. I don't like falling. Wow! Now my legs are done. It felt so good to be able to ride and walk a little bit. Thank You babe!"

"You're welcome,Breezy. Now get out there and show them how it's done. I will be watching from thesidelines."

"You got it. Tonight is for you babe."

It was the last of the rodeo and the bull ridingstarted. T. J pulls Triple Threat, Hoss has pulledBrutis, Jose pulled Little Jake, J. C has pulled Diablo. "Mommy, no. He will kill Uncle J. C."

"Jeremy, he is the money bull. You know that."

"I know, Mom but none of our riders have pulled him until now."

"I got an idea. Is Mara still tacked up?"

"I think so. Good!Come on, Jeremy. Help me."

"Okay!"said Jeremy as Sabrina tightened the girth on both her horses.

"Mommy, what are we doing?"

"Put all your weight on WaKeyA's other stirrup."

"Okay I am up."

"Now you get on Mara."

"Oh! We are going out to ride."

"You got it. All you have to do is get his attention once J. C is down. If J. C gets hung up I will get beside him while you stop him. For now we just let J. C ride it out. Okay? Now, let's go watch Daddy ride."

"Okay let's go." That was a solid ride for T. J Avery with a score of 94 well he's going to be hard to beat. "Sabrina what are you doing?"

"T. J just hush and get on your horse and come help us."

"Okay. I hope you know what you are doing."

"Trust us we do."

As J. C prepared to ride, Sabrina, T. J and Jeremy enter the arena. They excuse the other out riders. J. C doesn't even notice them in the arena. He gives the go-ahead and the gate swung open. Jeremy is on the other side of Sabrina so as to not distract Diablo yet. After three seconds J. C is in trouble. He was thrown from side to side like a rag doll. "Come on, Jeremy. Work your magic. T. J, you take the right. I'll get the left. Got it? Let's go."

"Debo, Debo." Jeremy called out. "It's me, Jeremy."

"Sing, Jeremysing."

"Mommy, I have to mount his head. It's uncle's only chance."

"Goahead.. Keep singing as you do. Jump, Jeremy jump. Now!"

"That kid must be crazy. He is on that bull's head."

"Debo, I won't let go!"

"Stop it before you hurt your boy."

"This light of mine. I'm gonnA let him shine. That's it boy. Settle down it's me. Let Mommy cut the rider off of you. Mom, talk to him. "

"Diablo, it's me baby. I'll have him loose in no time. Okay, he's free. Jeremy, slide back. We will get him out so the medics can get in."

"Okay, Mom lets go."

"Come on Mara follow us. T. J stay with J. C Please. I" got him."

"Good job Jeremy."

"Mom, I am gonna stay with Debo for a few."

"Okay. Bring Mara when you come."

"I got her boss."

"Thanks Hoss. I am glad you're here I think I will need help down."

"I got you. Now, that you are down and in your chair- are you crazy?! You and my nephew could have been killed!"

"No, we're not crazy. We knew exactly what we were doing. Don't criticize or I will let Jeremy pull his bull completely. You forget that is Jeremy's baby. He saved him when that bull would have otherwise died."

"Okay you're right. You win this time.

"Now let's go check on J. C then see how Jeremy is doing with Diablo."

"Good idea. Let's go. Hey can I push you?"

"Do I look stupid? Don't answer that. No, you can't push me. I am fine Thank you,"

"Hey T. J. How is J. C?"

"Well, he came to. He says he never wants to ride Diablo again. I didn't have the heart to tell him you and his nephew saved him."

"Good don't we wouldn't want him to know Jeremy can out ride him."

"Sabrina, you're bad."

"No, just a little comedy helps every now and then. T. J we are headed to check on Jeremy and Diablo you coming?"

"Yeah, lets go."

"Jeremy, you two okay?"

"No, Mom. Dad, we need to move him. He's out again for a while."

"What's wrong, Jeremy?"

"Come here Mom. Look, he's been cut underneath where the rope goes."

"What thehell?!. T. J look at this. Hoss, get me the rope that was on him."

"Okay. Be right back."

"Sabrina, we don't have any ropes that would do that."

"I know we don't. Jeremy let's put him between WaKey A and Mara. He's comfortable with them."

"Good idea, Mom. That's why he wouldn't listen to me at first."

"Okay just get him moved."

"T. J, Sis look. The rope has been tampered with. It has razors in it. I don't know who would have done something like that but it's cruel."

"I think I may know. If I am right I will personally see to it their whole crew is permanently banned from any and all rodeos nationwide for life. They will never work in or around animals again. Meanwhile I am going to hire a full-time guard to protect him."

"Sabrina, don't you think you are going overboard a bit?"

"No. I am not. You explain to your son why his bull is dead when someone possessions (?) his bull."

"Okay you win. You can hire security for Diablo."

"Thankyou."

"Okay T. J. Now that Diablo has security and I have cameras on him, let's go back to the hotel. I am worn out."

"Good idea. Let's go. Hopefully the ladies have the children bathed, fed and in bed."

"Trust me they will."

# CHAPTER 24

The next morning Sabrina awakened to find herself snuggled up to T. J. He seems so peaceful sound asleep. Sabrina decided to wake him with sweet kisses. She started by gently kissing his sweet lips then nibbled his ear. Next, she kissed his neck working her way down. She soon finds he is erect. She then decided to gently suckle his erection. Now that he is very erect she slid her way up on top of him. She kissed him then started to lower herself on to him. As he enters her Sabrina moans with satisfaction. The two of them enjoy sweet romance as they begin to climax at the same time.

After they have finished, Sabrina lay in his arms smiling. "Wow, Breezy! You haven't done that in a very long time. Thank you sweetheart! That was fabulous."

"T. J I just wanted to let you know in my own way how much I still love you."

"Breezy, I think we need to romance each other like that more often."

"No doubt. But it's your turn next time T. J."

"Not a problem, sexy. We can now make love like that with no worries about you getting pregnant."

"I think it is more fun now."

"Babe it seems as though I got even harder."

"T. J honey I think you may be onto something."

"This going to be great lovemaking at its best."

"T. J honey I have been thinking about some stuff."

"What's on your mind, darling?"

"Well, I think we need to purchase a bus-one that is customized for the kids. Skylar, Mom, and Margy will ride with them. They can kind of be at home on the bus. The bus will roll with us and keep the kids taken care of."

"Good idea, babe. Let's get dressed and go find one."

"Okay but we have another issue. I think we are going to need another truck as well."

"Okay Breezy. I think you're right. Now that the pens have came in, we will be needing a driver that can help tear down and set up. What do you think about hiring a company that has a driver? I think this way we won't be totally responsible for that extra truck and driver."

"Sabrina, I take it you have a company in mind."

"Well yes and no. I have checked out three different ones. There is one that stands out the most."

"Well Bree, get in touch with them and we will see what they have to offer. Now let's go find ourselves a bus."

At the bus dealer Sabrina kept going back to one bus. She thinks she has found the perfect bus. So far she has only gotten to look in through the windows. She is hoping that she is correct about what she sees. A salesman approached them. "Good morning can I help you with something."

"Yes I want to see the inside of this bus."

"Ma'am I don't think you can afford this one. Let me show you some the others."

"No. I want to see this one."

"Ma'am this one is really pricey."

"T. J, why don't you go with him and look?"

"Okay, whatever you want babe. You're the boss."

Sabrina wheeled herself into the office. "Hello. Can I see a manager please?"

"Yes ma'am."

A well dressed man walks out. "Hello. I am Bill. How can I help you?"

"Well Bill, I am Sabrina. I asked to look at a certain bus outside. Your salesman would not show it to me. He insisted I couldn't afford it. Will you please let me see that bus?"

"Yes ma'am. Let me get my keys." Sabrina was shown the bus that she wanted to look at. She climbs in and is amazed. She was right it's what she wants and then some. "Well how much do you want for it?"

"Well this bus was built for a singer but, she backed out at the last minute."

"Well give me a price."

"Well it was at 750,000. I think I can go lower if your credit goes through."

"Let's go somewhere and talk."

Back in Bill's office, Sabrina starts talking,. "Okay Bil.l I know the game. I know that the price you gave me is a total large mark-up."

"Yes ma'am it is written up."

"Well here's what I am offering. I will give you 500,000 for it. I know it's been driven. It has 1000 miles on it already. What I am offering is tax tags and title out the door. Oh yeah and I have the cash on me."

"You drive a hard bargain. Okay we can do it. Let's get the paper work together."

"Yeah, lets!" tThis money is blowing a hole in my pocket." Sabrina handed him the cash and signed thepaperwork.. He turned over the keys to her. "Thank you, Bill. It's been great dealing with you. Here are some tickets for you and your family. Come on out and enjoy the show."

"I think we will. Thank you, Sabrina."

Sabrina wheeled herself out to T. J. "Hey babe are you ready to go?"

"Yes if want to. Oh! By the way, here catch! I bought that bus."

"How did you do that?, the salesman asks.

"I went over your head and bought it. We paid cash. I have a tip for you, son. Never underestimate anyone. In other words, don't judge a book by its cover. I had cash on me. You just didn't give me a chance."

"Can you drive the car back?"

"No. They are hooking it up to the bus as we speak."

"Okay that works. I was wondering how you was going to pull that one off."

"Well now you know."

"That's another reason I love you so much babe. You always think ahead."

"Okay T. J now that we are out of there we need to discuss hiring a truck and driver that can and will travel with us."

"Well Breezy, what do you have in mind?"

"Well I have looked at several companies. So far there is only one that can fill our needs and can start right awaywhen we start tearing down tomorrow night. The driver can be here to get started. We will have exclusive use of truck and driver for the rest of the tour."

"Okay Breezy. Tell me more about the company."

"Like what?"

"Well, the name of the company, the type of truck, maybe some background on the driver. You know, those kinds of things."

"Well let me call them back and I will have all of it for you."

"Okay." Sabrina called up the company and set a meeting with the company later that day.

## CHAPTER 25

While the bus was taken to the arena, T. J and Sabrina headed to Nile, Illinois. They have a 3:00 p.m appointment with the owner of the company. "Sabrina, what is the name of the company where we are going? "Windy City Carriers. They are a small to medium company. They seem to take pride in being a family-oriented company."

"Good. Because that means they also take pride in their drivers and equipment. That's the way I understand it. Looks like we are here."

Theyparked and got out. As they entered the building, they were met by a lovely lady. She introduces herself as Neva, the owner's wife. "Dan will be along in a few. He is wrapping things up inside. Would you like to see the truck that will be assigned to work for you?"

"Sure that would be great!"

"Here we have a new Volvo 760. It's set up to run 75mph. It has a Volvo engine and the driver will have all the comforts of home inside. It is pulling a new Great Dane trailer."

"Nice, very nice."

"There's Dan now."

"Hello I am Dan. I take it my wife has showed you the equipment."

"Yes she has. Thank you."

"Now would you like to go somewhere that we can sit and talk?"

"Sure."

They follow Dan to a small restaurant where they all go inside and sit down. After they have ordered, they begin talking.

"Well do you have any questions for me?"

"Yes a few come to mind. First, we need to know if you have made your driver aware that they will be traveling with the rodeo circuit?"

"Yes and he is pretty excited about it."

"Next question, how much experience does he have?"

"Going on twenty years now, five of it has been with us."

"Would you consider him to be a good driver?"

"Of course. We only hire and employ some of the best. He is also very considerate around women and children. We thought about that before we decided on the right driver for this job. Seeing as how he will be around many women and children with the rodeo."

"Thank you. Not many people take that into consideration."

"You are more thanwelcome."

"Tell us about the driver you have lined up? Like how old is this gentleman? Does he require any home time? Is he willing to help with tearing down and setting up equipment; loading and unloading his truck? It is mainly gates for the animals… things of this nature."

"He is 52yrs old. He knows he will be expected to help with things of that nature. His name is Patrick. He's a big guy with loading and unloading in his background. We all call him Pat."

"When can he start? Tonight, if you want."

"That would be great. Let him know that besides what he earns with you we will taking care of some of his expenses. Like most of the time, our crew eats together. He will become like family to us."

"Okay. I will send him your way this evening then."

Now headed back to the rodeo T. J and Sabrina are pleased with their day. "T. J I am so glad we hired Windy City Carriers to help us on the circuit. That truck and trailer says professionalism. Plus I liked what they had to say about their driver. He seems like he will fit in great with our crew."

"Me too Breezy. I hate it when you are right. This time I am glad that you where right though. You never take anything for granted. You always know the right questions to ask."

"Not always. Just when it comes to keeping my loved ones safe."

"Are you riding tonight, Breezy?"

"No I am exhausted. I think I will just relax the rest of the evening."

# CHAPTER 26

It has now been six weeks since Pat with Windy City Carriers was hired on. He always seems to get ahead of them. By the time they arrive with the animals, he is half done setting up. Sabrina decided to tell him how grateful they are. They are now setting up in San Diego. They have arrived two days ahead of schedule. "Hey Pat. I have noticed you always seem to get way ahead of us."

"Yes you need places set up to unload when you arrive."

"True and I just wanted to say thank you. I also thought you might like to have a little extra time to yourself for a change. You might want to go get yourself a steak dinner," said Sabrina as she handed Pat a gift card.

"Really? Are you sure?"

"Yes or I wouldn't have just handed you that gift card."

"Yes, I will enjoy the dinner. I still need to help a little more with this bull shoots though. I have the pins that hold them together in a certain order."

"Okay, suit yourself."

"Hey boss lady, when are we going to start using Diablo again?"

"We're not. He is going home to become one of our main breeding stock. I can't take a chance of someone doing something stupid to him again. He has been through too much. Plus, I fear he will end up killing someone."

"You mean Lance?"

"Wel,l yes. That's one that he would kill in a heartbeat if he could get to him. I don't think Jeremy would even be able to stop him. Diablo hates Lance with a passion and with good cause though. I still believe Lance was the one who messed with that bucking strap. I just can't prove it."

"Do you think you will ever barrel race again? How about even be able to drive your semi again?"

"I am hoping to be able to do both again. I just don't know when. I still don't have enough feeling back in my legs. I don't feel confident enough to do either as of yet. I really miss both. I know Wa Key A doesn't mind he is getting a bit lazy if you ask me. Mara, on the other hand, seems to be getting a little wild. She wants to just go. She doesn't seem to be one that likes to be cooped up. I was thinking about letting her out in the arena tonight. Let her run and get it out of her system."

"Sounds good. Let me know. I will help you put her out."

"Okay, J. C will "do.

Later that evening Sabrina is sitting by the entrance to the arena watching Mara run a buck. Mara seemed to be enjoying herself. Sierra walks up. "Hi Sabrina. How are you this evening?"

"Bummed a little bit, I guess."

"Why? What's wrong?"

"I know in my heart this little girl misses me riding her. I just can't though. Not yet, not the way she needs me to. Not the way I need to in order to barrel race her. I still don't have full use of my legs. She is such a great horse and very quick. I only hope letting her out like this helps take the edge off. She was getting pretty hyper from being cooped up."

"It seems she is having a good time."

"Yeah I see that."

"Hey I have an idea!"

"What might that be?"

"Well, you know I have had to pull in the last two events. My boy totally pulled a muscle. The vet says he can't run this weekend either. Would you consider letting me run Mara for you?"

"She can be a handful. She has her quirks."

"Okay you can teach me. We still have a couple of days. We can practice early before anyone else starts moving about."

"I guess we could try. It wouldn't hurt to see if she will accept you."

"Okay. Hpw about 8:00 tomorrow morning?"

"Okay, but you better bring some carrots."

"Bribery. I can do that. Let's start now. You bring her in and brush her down. We will see how she reacts to that."

"Okay I got it."

They have accomplished a good brushing. "See you in the morning."

"See you then. Thanks Sabrina!"

# CHAPTER 27

It has been several weeks since Sabrina started letting Sierra ride Mara. Now that her horse is sound, Sierra tell Sabrina she plans to go back to riding her own horse to finish out the rodeo. Sabrina fully understands. She thanks Sierra for helping settled Mara down. Everything seems to be closing up fast now as the season winds down. T. J didn't do too great because he took so long off with Sabrina and the kids. Jose on the other hand is ahead in the bareback bronc riding while Hoss is 2 points ahead in the bull riding. The saddle bronc is being dominated by a young man from North Carolina. Barrel racing is a close match with Sierra and Britney. There are only two more events then the season will be over.

"T. J, I think I want to take the kids, Skylar, Mom, and Margy home to the ranch. The only thing is I plan to take my truck and bull rack. I will be taking the ponies, my two horses and Diablo with me. Then I will drive my pick-up truck back. If you want I can take a few of the other bulls that we haven't been bucking with me as well."

"Honey are you sure you are up to it?"

"Yeah I am sure."

"How about you get Pat to go with you in case you need him to drive?"

"I got this. I wouldn't have mentioned it if I didn't feel I could do it."

"I know but I worry. I love you, Breezy. I already almost lost you once this year."

"Okay. If it will make you happy, he can ride along with me."

"Thank you, baby!"
"You'rewelcome!"

Now that Sabrina has seen to everything at the ranch, sheand Pat head back to Tucson to the rodeo. They talk while they drive along. "So how do you like running with us?"

"It's been exciting. I can't believe how gentle all those animals really are. Are you really retiring that big bull?"

"Yes he's not as gentle as he seems."

"Okay. But your oldest handled him very well."

"Those two made a connection a long time ago. He has it in for one of the riders on the circuit. It's a long story. I fear Diablo will kill Lance if given the chance. He hates him worse than anything I have ever seen. The bull does have his reasons though and they are good ones. Lance has done some very cruel things to him. I will say no more about it."

"Okay I understand."

"You do know you're welcome with us anytime."

"Thanks. I appreciate it."

"Tell you what if we need a driver again next year we will call and ask for you."

"That works and I will be glad to help if you need me."

They arrive back at the arena, the rodeo is over for the evening. They will ride tomorrow then pack up and head for home. Everyone can't wait to get home and relax for a while.

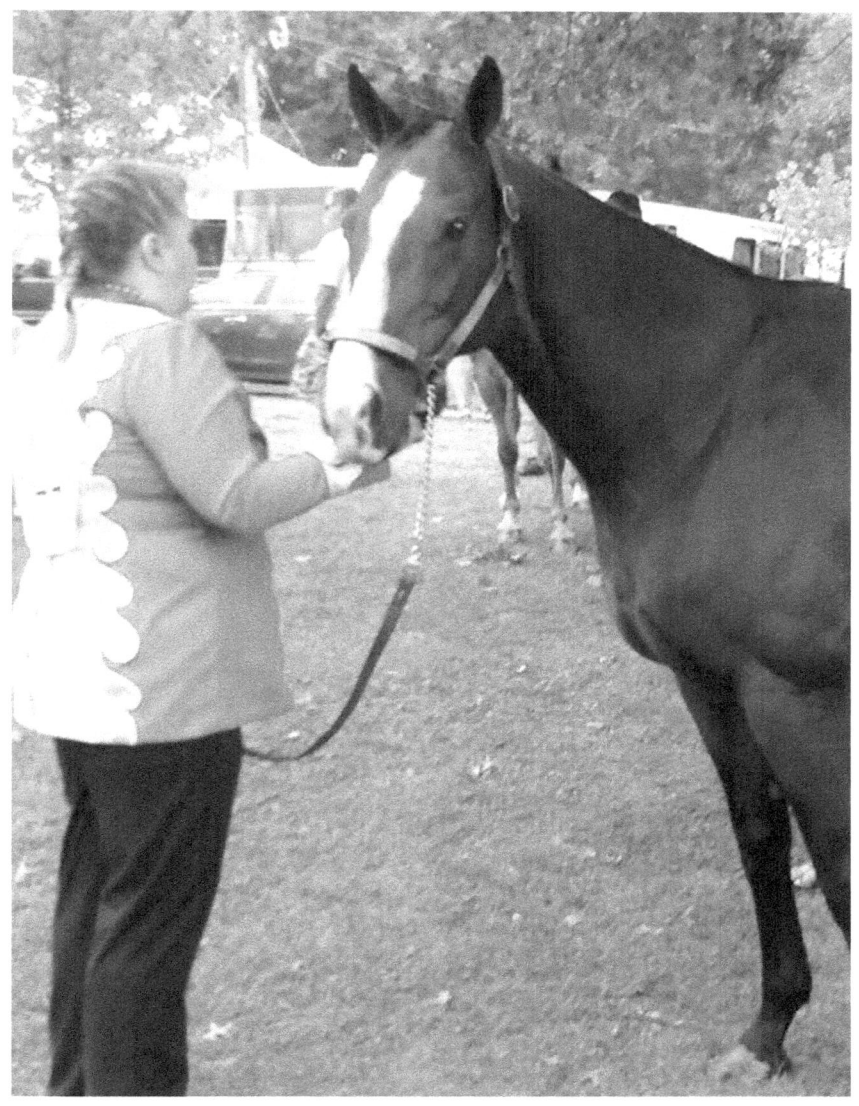

# H.MR. HART

# 18 WHEELS RODEOS AND BULLS

*In memory of Sony Boy's Midnight.
His last professional show. Ridden by H.M.R Hart*

www.ingramcontent.com/pod-product-compliance
Lightning Source LLC
LaVergne TN
LVHW011729060526
838200LV00051B/3086